Love Means...

FREEDOM

ANDREW GREY

Dreamspinner Press

Published by
Dreamspinner Press
4760 Preston Road
Suite 244-149
Frisco, TX 75034
http://www.dreamspinnerpress.com/

Love Means… Freedom

Cover Design by Mara McKennen

ISBN: 978-1-61581-517-3

Printed in the United States of America
First Edition
July, 2010

eBook edition available
eBook ISBN: 978-1-61581-518-0

To my beta reader Gabi for all her help and insight.

Love Means ... Freedom

CHAPTER 1

THE truck pulled off the side of the road, skidding to a stop. "I don't need no freeloaders. If you won't pay, you can walk!" the man growled as Stone began reaching for the handle. "You should have just sucked it!"

Stone opened the passenger door and made a grab for his bag, figuring the driver would try to steal his stuff. He was right, because the truck began to move as soon as his foot hit the ground. Stone swiped his arm at the driver and hit him on the side of the face, the truck jerking to a stop again. Grabbing his bag and yanking, he tugged it with him and fell away from the truck as it took off again. "Old fucker," he yelled at the taillights, "I wouldn't suck that button mushroom dick of yours for nothing!" He did have some standards, after all. Watching the taillights disappear, he pulled himself out of the snow bank and stomped the snow off his clothes. "Damn, it's cold out here." He stomped a few times to get warm before picking up his pack and slinging it over his shoulder. He'd only been in the truck a few minutes, so he hadn't had much of a chance to warm up in the first place. He tried to figure his chances of getting lucky with a ride twice on a night like this.

Snow swirled around him as he began walking. Stone had no idea where he was going and only hoped he could find a warm place out of the wind, which began to pick up almost as soon as it began getting dark. He heard the sound of a car approaching behind him and put out his thumb, but the driver continued down the road, his wheels throwing up a wave of ice and slush, making Stone even colder. "Fuck." He rummaged around in his pack, but couldn't find his gloves. "God damn," he half cried to the silent trees, his adrenaline-fueled bravado popping like a soap bubble. He'd left his gloves in the old fuck's truck. He shoved his hands back in his pockets for warmth. "Maybe I should have just sucked him off." The thought made him shudder as tears threatened. He might have been desperate, but he wasn't that desperate, not yet. Wiping his eyes, he looked around at the darkening landscape of trees and white. "Maybe I will be soon." Huddling to keep his skin out of the wind, he continued walking and found himself approaching a corner.

Stone saw a sign that read, "West Shore Community College," and he began walking down the drive, figuring he could at least huddle in a doorway. The place looked shut tight and no one appeared to be around. As he walked, the trees formed a windbreak, giving him some relief, anyway.

Dark brick buildings came into view nearby, and he headed over to one of them, trying the door, but it was locked. Stone walked all around the building, but it was shut tight. He let out a sigh. He should have known; they were probably still on Christmas break and wouldn't be back for a while. He thought about breaking a window, but with his luck, the place would be alarmed. Maybe at least jail would be warm.

He actually picked up a stone and was about to hurl it toward a sheet of glass when he saw lights flickering between the trees. Lights meant people and maybe warmth. Putting down the rock, he headed toward the lights, hoping he'd get lucky.

Stone broke out of the trees and the wind cut right through his coat. He looked ahead and saw what appeared to be the outline of a barn and farmhouse. Walking across the street, he trudged through the snow and up to the front porch, now shivering with every step, praying they'd maybe let him sleep in their barn. Pulling his hand out of his pocket, he rapped on the screen door, his hand tingling as it woke a little before going numb again, and he shoved it back in his pocket.

Heavy footsteps approached and the door opened, and Stone opened his mouth to speak, but his teeth only chattered and he began to shake.

"Eli!" the man yelled into the house, "I need help!" The first man was joined by another, and the door opened further. Stone thanked his lucky stars as he was ushered into the warm room, the door closing behind him.

He stood on the mat and shivered, eyes closed as he let the warmth embrace him. Hands began to remove his coat and he jerked away forcefully. "Hey, kid. No one's going to hurt you. We just need to get this off so you can get warm." Stone opened his eyes and looked at the man trying to help him with his coat. "What's your name?"

"S... S... Stone," he stammered through chattering teeth. "Stone Hillyard."

"I'm Geoff and this is Eli. We just need to get your coat off."

Stone let his arms fall to his side and felt his coat slip from his body, the warmth of the house reaching through his shirt to his skin, and he couldn't suppress a sigh.

"Take your shoes off and come sit on the sofa," Eli said softly.

"T... t... thanks." Somehow Stone got his shoes off and walked barefoot to the sofa. He heard a gasp and then someone hurried up a set of stairs. Stone didn't really care what happened; he just knew he needed to get warm somehow. He heard feet descend the stairs at a run, and then he was enveloped in a big, puffy, warm quilt and he began to shake in earnest.

"Adelle," he heard Geoff call into another room as he pulled the quilt up around his ears, which were starting to burn as the feeling returned.

"Mr. Geoff." He saw an older black woman walk into the room. "What happened?"

"I found him on the doorstep. Would you make him something hot? We need to get him warm. I think he may have frostbite, I know he's close to hypothermia." She hurried away, and Stone breathed a sigh of relief as his body shook and his feet throbbed with pain as the feeling returned. His hands tingled as well, but at least he could still feel those.

The woman returned, and he tried to take the mug she offered, but his hands couldn't grip it well and it almost slipped from his hands. "It's okay, darling, I got it." She took the mug again and held it to his lips. "Just a few sips to start with."

The liquid burned a little as it went down, and then he began to feel some warmth on the inside. He tried to drink more, but she pulled the mug back. "Take it easy. Too much will shock yer system." He nodded, and she waited a few minutes before bringing the mug to his lips again. This time, he was able to drink a gulp, and it went down smooth and warm.

"Mmmm." Hot chocolate had never tasted so good in his life, and he took another drink and then reached for the mug, the warmth seeping into his hands. The tingling subsided and he felt the burning in his feet start to dissipate. "Thank you." He took a few more drinks and emptied the mug, closing his eyes as the thick liquid slid down his throat and hit his empty stomach, which growled loudly at being teased.

"When was the last time you ate?" The woman fussed over him as other people came in the room, and he heard questions being asked and answered in hushed tones. Stone shrugged and looked into the four male faces that stood around the sofa. "You boys scoot and let me take care of him," the woman scolded.

Love Means ... Freedom

"Let's get everything closed up for the night; it's going to be very cold," Geoff said, and the men walked away, one of them making his way carefully upstairs.

"It's okay, sweetie, you're safe for now. Just relax and get warm, I'll be right back." She walked away and he heard her working in the kitchen, humming softly to herself. She returned with a sandwich on a plate, and Stone found himself lifting one half and biting into it. After he swallowed, he finished the rest in a single bite and took the other half. "Lord, slow down. No one's going to take it from ya." Stone looked up at her smiling face and tried to take smaller bites, but his stomach screamed for more. When the sandwich was gone, another appeared, and Stone pushed down the tears that threatened to come to the surface. "There, there, just eat your fill."

After three sandwiches and another big mug of hot chocolate, he was finally full and couldn't keep his eyes open any more. "Thank you, ma'am."

She took the plate and mug. "You're welcome. Now just rest and I'll be right here."

Stone closed his eyes and found himself floating. Music invaded his mind and memories he'd thought long gone came back to him. Images of his mother dancing around the living room with him, the two of them dancing happily, flashed through his dreams.

Stone's eyes cracked open. He must have dozed off, but the music was still there. He recognized the tune as he listened, his breathing evening out again. He was truly warm and full—feelings he hadn't felt in a long time. Closing his eyes again, he felt himself fall into a deep, restful sleep.

IT WAS dark when he woke again. He felt, rather than heard or saw, someone else in the room with him, but he didn't want to move. Shifting on the sofa, he found a comfortable spot and drifted back to sleep, figuring he had to be dreaming. And if he was, he didn't want to wake up, ever. Maybe he was dead and this was Heaven.

When he woke again, there were other people in the room, but it was still dark. Huffing softly, he shifted, and the cocoon of warmth around him began to shift. The room quieted again, but now he was wide awake. Looking around, he saw a man sitting in a chair, running his fingers over the pages of a book.

"I'm Robbie. Are you hungry?" He put the book carefully on the table next to the chair and got to his feet, walking to the sofa, reaching it, and Stone felt a hand glance along his leg. "There you are."

"You're blind." The realization was surprising to Stone.

"Last time I looked, yeah." Robbie laughed and Stone joined him. It felt good to laugh; he hadn't done it in a while. "Are you hungry?" Stone nodded and pushed back the blanket, his bare feet hitting the cool floor. "I can't hear your head moving. Nothing rattles." Stone saw Robbie's smile and knew he was playing with him.

"Sorry, yes."

"Then come in the kitchen, I'm sure Adelle will have something hot for you." Stone watched as Robbie led the way, and he marveled at how easily he moved through the house. Robbie turned toward him and scowled. "Are you barefoot?"

Stone felt his cheeks color with shame. "Yeah."

"Go on in the kitchen and I'll get you some socks." Stone watched as Robbie turned and made his way up the stairs.

When he disappeared from view, Stone went into the kitchen and found Adelle working at the counter, humming to herself. "Was that you who stayed with me?"

She stopped working and turned around. "I wanted to make sure you were all right." She motioned toward the table. "Sit down and I'll bring you some pancakes." She turned away, and Stone felt his mouth start to water, and he wondered what the hell was happening to him. These people barely knew his name, yet they were treating him so nice.

Love Means ... Freedom

He didn't know what to make of it, but he figured they'd want something from him eventually.

A plate stacked high with hotcakes was placed in front of him, along with maple syrup and butter. The smell was almost too much, and he looked over at Adelle to make sure these were all for him, but she'd already gone back to work, so he poured syrup on the stack and ate until he thought he was going to burst, finally pushing back the empty plate. "Thank you, ma'am. That was delicious."

"You want some more?" She looked down at the plate that looked like it had been vacuumed clean.

"No, thank you." She took the plate and Stone pushed back from the table. Getting up, he went back into the living room and found his shoes, slipping them on his feet. Stone found his bag sitting on a chair along with his coat and even a pair of gloves. Stone slipped on his coat and swung his pack over his shoulder. He needed to get out of these nice peoples' way.

"Are you going to leave without saying good-bye?"

Stone turned and saw the blind man looking at him, which was really strange.

"I think it's best I get out of everyone's way. They don't need me mooching off them. Tell them thank you for me." Stone looked around the room. He wanted to remember this place. It wasn't often that people were as nice to him as these people had been, but he knew they definitely wouldn't want him around, not after everything.

"Why don't you let them make that decision?"

Stone stopped in his tracks and almost slipped the pack off his shoulder, almost. "They don't need me around. I'm no good for anybody." Stone heard a door bang shut, and then voices drifted in from the kitchen and got louder.

"You're up." Stone looked over and saw Geoff—he thought it was Geoff, anyway—standing in the kitchen doorway.

"Thanks for everything. I'll get out of your hair now." Stone moved toward the front door and opened it, stepping outside and pulling the door closed behind him. The cold bit into him almost as badly as it had the night before, and he hurried toward the street.

"Do you think this is a smart idea?" Stone stopped and turned around, seeing Geoff standing on the front porch. "It isn't any warmer this morning than it was last night."

Stone looked around, already starting to shiver. What in the hell was wrong with him? Slowly, he turned around and walked back toward the house and warmth. Geoff stepped aside and followed him back inside. Stone dropped his pack by the door, but left his coat on and followed Geoff into another room with a desk and a lot of strange machines that seemed to be turning out paper with bumps on them.

"Would you like to tell me why you were out in the cold alone last night?"

Stone shrugged. How he came to be outside alone was the last thing he wanted to talk about. Hell, his whole life was something he'd like to forget. "You've been very nice, but you don't want me around."

"Why don't you let me be the judge of who I want around my farm and family?" Geoff's face was firm, and Stone found himself fidgeting under Geoff's gaze.

"What the hell." Stone sank into a chair, pulling the zipper open on his coat, but ready to make a quick getaway if he had to. "I grew up on a small farm outside Petoskey. It was just my dad and me." Stone felt tears threaten, but he blinked them back and let his anger take over, pushing back the sadness, and to his surprise his voice firmed as well and he was able to go on. "I thought the old bastard loved me. It was only the two of us after my mother died."

"What happened?" Geoff's voice sounded so concerned, but Stone knew that would change.

"My old man kicked me out." The emotions threatened again, but he pushed them back, letting the love that had turned to hate keep him

Love Means ... freedom

strong. "So I guess he didn't love me after all." Stone looked at Geoff's eyes and saw them soften as he waited.

"You didn't answer my question." Stone heard a note of compassion in the farmer's voice and decided to go for broke.

"I told him I was gay." Stone watched Geoff's reaction, waiting to see what would happen. At best, he figured he'd be told to leave. At worst, he'd make a hasty retreat before he got hit like his old man had done to him so many times. The bruises were gone, but he could still feel the ache in his shoulder where the man had practically ripped his arm out of the socket as he threw him out of the house.

Geoff didn't say anything, and Stone watched as the farmer got to his feet and walked toward him. *Okay, here it comes.* He expected to get hit, or to have him demand what the guy from the truck had. What he didn't expect was to get pulled to his feet and hugged, tight and hard. The strong man didn't make any sort of move. He wasn't felt up, he was just comforted—the way Stone had hoped his own father would have comforted him. "No one will hurt you here." The words reached Stone's ears, and he raised his arms and put them around the man, returning the hug. This was the first comfort of any kind he'd received since he'd been thrown out.

The grip lessened and Geoff stepped back, and Stone's legs practically gave out as he slumped back into the soft chair. "How long have you been on your own?"

"About three months. For a while I was able to work cutting Christmas trees for a friend. But the job ran out, so I started heading south, figuring I'd try to get somewhere warm. The money ran out and I tried hitching."

"You said you grew up on a farm?"

"Yeah." Stone was starting to get suspicious. "We raised pigs." Stone shuddered. The last thing he ever wanted to do again was have anything to do with pigs.

"You willing to work?"

9

"Are you offering me a job? This time of year?" Winter was when most farms tended to go to sleep and needed less help, not more. "I don't want charity."

"I'm not offering charity, but hard work. I need someone to keep the barn clean. The guy who was doing it went back to school and we've been making do. I've got twenty stalls that need to be kept clean and a tack room that must be kept neat. You ever worked with horses?"

Stone nodded, hardly able to believe his luck. Instead of getting beaten up, he was being offered a job. "I learned how to ride when I was a kid." He'd had to leave his horse behind when his dad kicked him out, and his heart ached that he hadn't been able to take Buster with him. "Had a horse of my own." Damn it, he was starting to act like a girl, sniffling and everything.

"Good. My partner, Eli, gives riding lessons, and if it works out, he may have you help him."

Stone could hardly believe his ears. "Your partner?" He saw Geoff nod. Stone thought for a while. "Is he the man I saw last night when you answered the door?" He got another nod and a smile. "Then who's the blind guy?" He saw Geoff scowl and realized he was being rude. "I mean Robbie, is he your brother?"

Geoff held up his hand. "After we're done here, I'll introduce you to everybody, but I need to know some things." Now it was Stone's turn to nod slowly. "How old are you?"

Stone's first inclination was to lie, but he didn't. "Nineteen." He heard Geoff growl deep in his throat and wondered what that was for and what he'd done wrong. Immediately he began to bite his lips with worry. Just when things were looking up....

"You have ID and things?"

"Yes, sir." He fumbled in his coat pocked for his worn wallet.

Geoff stood up again and extended his hand. "Then you have a job if you want it."

Stone could hardly believe it. Last night he'd almost frozen to death, and today he'd been offered a job on a farm owned by a gay couple. Hesitantly, he extended his hand and they shook. "You won't regret it."

Geoff released his hand and opened the office door. "Eli," Geoff said, and a man got up from the sofa. "This is Stone, and he's going to be working in the barn. He's got experience with horses." Stone alternated his gaze between the two men and relaxed when he saw the pleased look on Eli's face. "I believe you already know Robbie. He's my able assistant and our resident musician."

"That was you last night? I thought I was dreaming, it was so beautiful."

Robbie beamed at him. "Thank you." Stone watched as Robbie appeared to listen before turning toward Geoff. "Can I get started?"

"Certainly. I printed out what you'll need and it's on the embosser." Robbie smiled and made his way carefully into the office, closing the door.

"Is he"—Stone's voice lowered to a whisper—"gay too?"

He saw Geoff smile. "Yes. His partner Joey is out working, which is where we should be as well." Geoff looked down at his feet. "You'll need warmer boots and some thicker clothes."

"I'll find him some," Eli said before heading upstairs.

"I need to help Robbie. Eli will be right back down and we'll take you out so you can meet everyone else and get started." Geoff opened the office door, leaving Stone alone in the living room. Not knowing what else to do, he peered out the window. The snow from yesterday had stopped and the day was bright and clear. He could hardly believe his luck. He'd happened upon a farm owned by gay people in the middle of a snowstorm, and they'd offered him a job in addition to having kept him from freezing to death. Maybe, just maybe, his luck was changing. Footsteps on the stairs broke him out of his thoughts.

CHAPTER 2

"TAKE it easy. You shouldn't overdo it," the therapist warned as he watched Preston maneuvering himself between the bars.

"I want to walk!" Preston yelled as he gritted his teeth. "The fucking doctor said I'd never walk again," he grunted as he forced his legs to work. "I intend to walk up to that asshole and shake his hand," he said as he moved again, "or punch the fucker's face!" He reached the end and turned around, collapsing into the wheelchair. "I do intend to walk again." He looked at the therapist and grinned, saying, "Sorry, Jasper, I didn't mean to take it out on you." The anger and frustration slipped away as he wheeled himself toward the door. "I just want this so badly."

"I know you do, and so do I, but injuring yourself isn't going to make it happen faster." Jasper held the door open. "You've come a long way in a short time."

"Not far enough." Preston was determined and naturally impatient.

"Pres," his physical therapist and friend began, "your muscles are just now starting to get the blood they need to function. Sometimes you need to let things progress on their own, and they just won't be rushed."

Love Means ... *Freedom*

Preston whipped the chair around. "I thought therapists were supposed to be sadistic." A huge grin broke onto his face.

"I may be a sadistic therapist, but I'm also your friend. I want you to walk again; I just don't want you to hurt yourself doing it." Jasper led the way back into the lobby where Preston's mother was waiting for him.

Preston hated that at twenty-six, he was back living with his parents and dependent upon them again. A drunk driver had not only taken away the use of his legs but also his freedom, and he was determined above all else to get it back. Feeling had returned, and after numerous surgeries, some movement had returned. As soon as he could lift his legs, he'd started exercising when no one was around. "I'm ready to go, Mom."

"Okay, honey." She got to her feet and walked over to him, stepping behind the chair to push Preston to the car.

"I don't need any help," he snapped. She handed him his coat, and he shrugged it on before gripping the wheels and propelling himself forward, the doors opening automatically in front of him. "I just need to do things for myself." He jetted through the parking lot, stopping near the car and waiting for her to unlock the doors. Positioning the chair near the seat, he shifted himself onto his shaky, but strengthening, legs and onto the seat. He then folded the chair and maneuvered it behind his seat. Strapping himself in, he closed the door and fastened his seatbelt. "I'm sorry I yelled. It's just important that I do it myself."

"I know." She turned to him and smiled. "I just forget and want to help." She started the car and pulled out of the parking lot. Preston had to admit that his mom had been as good and supportive as he could have hoped. She'd carted him wherever he needed to go and took time off work so he could get to his therapy appointments. "Your father called. He'll be home in a few days."

"Oh goody." Preston actually whirled his finger in mock excitement. In stark contrast to his mother, Preston's father had seen his accident as yet another way he'd imposed himself on their lives. His father was the main reason he wanted to be out of the house. The man tended to be overbearing and self-centered on his best days.

"Pres, your father works hard," his mother soothed as they continued their drive toward the west, turning on Lake Drive.

"Don't defend him, Mom. Not to me." Preston's father had nearly had a stroke when he'd told him he was gay. After about a week, he began parading every girl he could find through the house because Preston "just hadn't met the right one yet." It was embarrassing for him and the girls when he told each one that he was gay. Eventually his father had stopped, but Preston knew he hadn't given up. Milford Harding the Third never gave up; he just bided his time before he struck again. It was only Preston's accident that had called a truce between them. "At least we have a few days of peace left."

His mother didn't respond, and they rode in silence until she pulled the car into the circular driveway before parking in the three-car garage. Preston opened the door and slid out his chair, opening it before climbing on and making his way to the back door, where a ramp led into the house.

The ramp was the only concession to his injury that he'd let his mother make. To her credit, she'd looked into elevators and adding lifts to the house, but Preston was determined that he wouldn't need the chair forever. So they'd moved his bedroom from the second floor to the first and that was it. "I'm going to lie down for a while." The therapy always made him tired. He wheeled himself to his room, turning before entering. "Thanks, Mom, for everything." He smiled at her. She smiled back and he knew everything was all right. He made a note that when this was over, he was going to do something very special for her. She deserved it.

He shifted himself out of the chair and onto the bed, covering himself and closing his eyes. He'd just started dozing off when his phone rang. He picked it up from the bedside table and smiled when he saw the name. "Hi, sexy." Preston beamed into the phone, everything else forgotten.

"How'd therapy go?"

He loved the sound of Kent's voice, always had. "Good. I was able to make it all the way this time."

"That's great." There was strain in his voice.

"Are we still going out tonight?" Preston had been looking forward to it all through therapy.

"That's what I was calling about." Kent's voice suddenly sounded strange.

"If you don't want to go out tonight, we can get together tomorrow."

"Preston, look, I don't think I can do this anymore."

Preston sat up in bed, using his hands to lift himself. "What are you saying?"

"It's over, Preston. I've met someone else."

"You selfish son of a bitch!" Tears threatened, but his anger held them back. "How long have you been sleeping around?"

"David and I have been seeing each other for a few weeks."

Preston didn't need to hear any more. He closed the phone and squeezed his eyes shut. He wanted to scream and throw the phone against the wall, but that wouldn't accomplish anything anyway. "How could I have been so stupid?" He knew he should have seen it coming, but he hadn't wanted to.

His phone rang again and he swore he was going to chuck it outside if it was Kent. It wasn't. "Hello."

"What's wrong? Are you okay?" Jasper's voice filled with concern.

"Kent just dumped me."

"I'm on my way." The phone went dead and he closed it, placing it on the table before lying back down. He covered himself up, but even in the warm room, he began to shiver. Closing his eyes, he let the tears come. Turning his face to the pillow so his mother couldn't hear, he wet the pillowcase as he let his pain run free.

He lost track of time, but eventually his door opened and then he felt a pair of hands on his shoulders turning him over before a tear-wavy Jasper pulled him into a hug. "Just let it go." Preston felt sadness wash over him as he did as Jasper said, letting the controls on his grief fall away. He heard a knock on his door, and Jasper moved slightly, but nothing more. Finally, as his tears subsided, Jasper pulled away. "What happened?"

Preston wiped his eyes. "We were supposed to go out tonight, but he called and told me he'd been seeing someone else."

"The bastard." Jasper shifted on the bed. "I always knew the man was an ass. I swear he was only dating you because of your dad and his money."

"Why didn't you tell me?" Preston shifted on the bed, trying to sit up again.

"Would you have listened?" Jasper waited for an answer, and Preston avoided his gaze. "I didn't think so." Then Jasper smiled. "But he's gone now."

"What are you so fucking happy about? Kent's gone and no one will ever look at me again!" He was about two seconds from throwing Jasper out, but the man just scoffed at him.

"Did you ever think that maybe this was a good thing? Maybe, just maybe, something good could come out this whole ordeal, and you might meet someone with something between his ears, unlike the vapid Kent."

"Like what? What good could come out of this? More sexy scars and additional therapy." He was being pissy, but he didn't care. Jasper

Love Means ... *Freedom*

got up from where he sat and glared down at him, and Preston thought he might have gone too far, but he really didn't give a fuck.

"You're way too caught up in the way that everyone looks, from their faces to their clothes. That's all you think matters." Jasper leaned closer, getting in Preston's face. "I've got a news flash for you, there's a whole big world out there of people who don't happen to be 'pretty.' Maybe it's time you developed more depth than an overturned saucer!" Preston was stunned into silence; he'd never heard his friend talk that way.

"I'm not that way," he protested feebly.

"When I met Derrick, you told me I should dump him, that I could do better. You remember that? Derrick, the man who stayed by your bedside with me the entire time you were in the hospital. The man who brought you home and carried you into this room, settled you in this bed." Jasper lowered his voice. "Remember when it hurt so bad you wanted to die and it was Derrick who held your hand and cried right along with you?" Preston nodded his head before lowering to look at the bedding. "He's the person I should have dumped because he isn't a muscle god or some pretty boy."

Had he really been that terrible? "Why didn't you say this before?"

"Because I kept hoping you'd grow out of it. Derrick is the most incredible person I've ever met, and he's beautiful because he loves me, truly loves me." Preston felt Jasper's hand slide into his. "There's nothing like waking up next to someone who truly loves you, and Kent never loved you, no matter what you might think. Because if he did, he'd be the one sitting where I am right now."

"Jesus." Preston swallowed. "Don't I get a little sympathy?"

"You've had enough sympathy for yourself to last a lifetime—it's time you got off your butt. I saw determination in you today, so take that and use it in the rest of your life. Kick Kent to the curb and find someone better, truly better."

17

"I knew you were a complete sadist." Preston smiled for the first time since Kent had called.

"Speaking of sadistic, I was calling you earlier because I found out about a new type of therapy I'd like you to try." Preston groaned, rolling his eyes, and Jasper slapped him on the shoulder. "This will be fun, I swear." He actually held up his hand. "There's a place between here and Scottville that does therapy riding. They'll put you on a horse and teach you how to ride. It's great exercise and it'll help you strengthen your legs."

"You've got to be kidding. I don't know the first thing about horses." But the idea did hold some interest. "Can they really get me on one of those big things?"

"Yes, and they'll teach you how to ride. It's worth a try, and it'll get you outside. They're certified, and I met the man who runs the program and his partner a few days ago. He's something else." Jasper set a card on the table near the bed. "Think about it."

"Did I hear you say partner? I assume you don't mean business partner."

Jasper smiled. "I mean the good kind of partner. The farm's owned by a gay couple as well. They're nice people. So you'll give it some thought?"

"Yeah." He looked up at Preston and said, "I promise."

Preston nodded his head, and Jasper pulled him into a hug. "You're going to be fine." Jasper got up and walked to the bedroom door. "Call me if you need anything." He opened the door. "Let's do something this weekend."

"Yeah." Preston was drained, but he felt better than he had in a while. Jasper raised his hand and then left the room, closing the door behind him.

His friend was right—but one thing at a time. He needed to get better, and that was only going to happen with hard work and therapy. Reaching to the table, he picked up the card, looking it over before dialing the number. "Laughton Farms," a male voice answered, "Robbie speaking."

Preston looked at the card. "I'm trying to reach No Boundaries Therapy Riding, but I think I have the wrong number."

"No, that's us as well. What can I help you with?"

"My therapist recommended that I call you. I was in an accident a few months ago and I'm just regaining the use of my legs. I can walk with help," he said, exaggerating a little, "and I was wondering if you would have room for me?"

"We're pretty full right now. Let me check a second." The phone was set down, and Preston heard someone moving around. "We don't have any group sessions available."

"I'd prefer private sessions." He didn't want to be on display for everyone anyway.

"Then when would you like to come out to see our facilities?"

"How about tomorrow at... uh... one?" If this would help, he figured the sooner the better.

"Can I have your name, please?"

"Preston Harding," he answered, and he waited while Robbie obviously wrote it down. "What should I wear?"

"Jeans and a warm shirt will be fine, along with a pair of boots if you have them, although that's not strictly necessary."

"I can do that." Preston had a closet full of clothes for every occasion.

"Thank you, we'll expect you tomorrow at one." The line disconnected, and Preston hung up the phone before sliding off the bed and back into his chair, gliding to the door. "Mom, will you be able to take me to therapy tomorrow at one?" He actually found himself smiling and looking forward to something new.

"Of course." She came around the corner and stopped, smiling. "What's got you so happy?"

"New kind of therapy." Preston answered.

"I thought you were excited about going out tonight." She wiped her hands on her dishtowel.

"Not going out." He swallowed as Kent's rejection hit him again. "Kent and I aren't seeing each other anymore. So I'm concentrating on walking again."

"Good. I never liked him." She looked relieved and more than a little pleased. "So what's the new therapy?"

"Riding horses." His mother's surprise made his smile even wider. "Why didn't you like Kent?"

Her eyes became firm. "He didn't love you." She swallowed and then continued. "Neither of us were thrilled when you told us you were gay, and I know your father has never accepted it, but I love you and want you to be happy. I can accept you being with a man as long as he loves you. Kent was just a freeloader."

Preston was shocked and pleased. He opened his arms, and she bent down so Preston could hug her. "Thank you, Mom."

She straightened up, her smile increasing. "So tell me all about this therapy, I used to ride horses, you know...." Preston followed her through the house and into the kitchen, the two of them talking, really talking, for the first time in months.

Love Means ... freedom

CHAPTER 3

STONE unzipped the coat that Eli had given him, letting it hang open for ventilation. The work kept him pretty warm, but cleaning stalls meant traveling outside constantly, and it was bloody cold outside. "You doing okay?" He heard a strange voice float over the wall of the stall. Turning, he saw a stranger standing in the doorway. "I'm Joey; you must be Stone. Geoff said I could find you in here."

Stone stopped mucking, leaning on the handle of the wide-bladed shovel. "I'd shake hands, but they're dirty."

Stone saw the man step into the stall, extending his hand anyway. "Don't care too much about that around here." Stone shook it, and then Joey looked around. "Nice job. I take it you've done this before?"

"Yeah, my dad and I had a small farm up north raising pigs. This is a whole lot easier and a good sight less smelly."

Joey smiled a bright smile and Stone noticed the faint scars on his face. "Sorry I didn't get to meet you yesterday, but I didn't get in until late and you were asleep."

Stone began shoveling again, figuring he could work while they talked. The last thing he wanted was for anybody to think he was a shirker. His daddy had raised him to work hard, and besides, Geoff had been good enough to give him this chance; there was no way he was gonna blow it. "I met your... um... partner, yesterday. He seems really nice." Stone threw a load of soiled bedding in the wheelbarrow.

"He is that." The voice came over the wall from the next stall. "Do you ride much?"

"Had horses most of my life; had to leave mine behind, though." Stone began working harder and making noise with the shovel, trying to discourage any further conversation on the subject.

"We've got a new therapy client in about a half hour. I'm getting Belle ready, and I was hoping you could help out." He heard the horse moving around and, when he wasn't shoveling, the light swish of the comb.

"Sure, just tell me what to do. I've never done therapy riding before."

"No sweat." The stall door closed, and he heard Joey's bootsteps as he finished cleaning out the stall, making a last run to the muck pile and returning with the first load of fresh bedding. Joey and Belle were moving around in the next stall, and he kept his mind on his work even though his body had been on overdrive since he'd been asked to stay. Robbie was cute, Joey was handsome and looked rather rugged even with the scars on his face, Geoff was incredibly handsome, and Eli was beautiful. Stone picked up the pace, using the work to get his mind off it. They were all taken, and he needed to keep himself under control.

When he finished up the stall, he heard the other stall door open, followed by the clomp of hooves on the barn floor. "Can you meet me in the ring in ten?"

"Sure," Stone called as he closed the door and put the tools away before walking through the barn and into the indoor, heated riding ring. The horse was hitched to a post, and Joey seemed to be checking out things, so Stone waited. A sound behind him drew his attention, and he saw a man rolling toward him in a wheelchair through the barn and then into the covered ring, followed by an older woman who Stone figured was his mother.

"Are you Preston?" Joey strode up to the man while Stone stayed behind with the horse. He watched as they talked for a while, and then Joey motioned for him to bring the horse to an area of the ring that sloped down and a sloping platform had been built. Combined, they allowed the rider to slide onto the horse. The man wheeled himself to the top of the ramp, and Stone watched those thick arms work as he lifted himself out of the chair and managed to stand. Joey helped the man get settled on the horse. "You did that very well."

"Thanks," the man mumbled from the top of the horse.

Joey continued, "Stone is going to lead you around the ring, and I want you to squeeze your legs around the horse. It'll help you stay on and keep your balance. I'll be right here, and all you need to do is wave if you feel like you might fall." Joey began adjusting the stirrups and making sure the man was comfortable. "Just relax and have fun." Joey stepped back, and Stone prepared to walk the horse around the ring.

"Are you ready?" Stone asked.

The man on the horse grunted something, and Stone began walking forward very slowly, circling the ring. Stone paid attention to the floor in front of him and where the horse was walking, trying to keep from looking at the man on the horse with the bright eyes and muscular chest and shoulders. "Hey, Stable Boy, do you think we can pick it up a bit?"

Stone turned and glared at the man. "My name is Stone." Before the arrogant ass could respond, he turned around and began walking faster.

"No too fast, Stone, he needs to get used to the horse," Joey called from across the ring. Stone slowed his steps slightly and kept walking. "Preston, try to move with the horse and use your legs."

Hearing his name again, Stone stifled a laugh. His mother might have named him after a soap opera character, but at least she hadn't given him a dweeby name like Preston.

"You need to use your legs if this is going to help you." Stone stopped as Joey walked up to the horse.

"I can't use my legs!" Stone was startled by the volume of Preston's voice and the vehemence behind it.

"Yes, you can. You stood so we could get you on the horse. The purpose of this therapy is to strengthen your legs." Joey began feeling Preston's legs, and Stone looked away. For a second he wondered what it would be like to feel those legs. He shook his head slightly; there was no way he was going to fantasize about Mr. Arrogant. "Grip the horse and you'll find it easier to stay on, and you'll actually feel something in your legs when you're done." Joey stepped away and Stone began moving again. "Much better." Joey said, complimenting Preston as Stone continued walking the horse around the ring.

"Hey, Stable Boy...."

Stone stopped abruptly and turned, glaring acidly at the rider. "My. Name. Is. Stone." He smirked. "Preston." He lilted his voice slightly and continued walking at the same pace. Preston kept taunting him and asking "Stable Boy" all kinds of questions whenever they were away from the others, but Stone just kept walking, pleased that he wasn't rising to the bait.

"So, Stable Boy...."

Stone took a deep breath and slowly released it. This guy's time had to be almost up.

"What do you do when you aren't leading horses around—shovel shit? Looks like you might have fallen into it."

He turned his head without stopping. "My name is Stone," he said through clenched teeth, "and if you don't stop with the stable boy crap, I'll beat the shit out of you—I don't care if you are some pathetic cripple in a wheelchair." He turned away and kept walking the horse. A few steps later, he couldn't help himself; he peeked back under the guise of checking on Belle and saw the devastated look on the rider's face before the expression changed and Preston's eyes blazed with hurt anger.

"Use your legs, Preston," Joey's voice reminded him. "That's it, you're doing great."

Stone's satisfaction lasted about two minutes, until his conscience took over and he began feeling guilty and a little concerned. What would Geoff think if he found out what he'd said? He almost turned to apologize, but he had some pride. Mr. Arrogant Preston, the bastard, had goaded him, and he deserved what he got. The man might be sort of cute, and Stone was pretty sure he was gay, but that didn't give him the right to be all superior and shit.

Joey signaled from the rail, and Stone walked Belle across the ring to the ramp, grateful that this was over. "I don't want to overdo it the first time," Joey began explaining as they approached the ramp. "Your legs might be sore, but that's because you were using muscles you haven't in a long time." Joey helped Preston off the horse and back into his chair. "Stone, would you please walk Belle back to her stall?"

"Sure, Joey." Grateful to be leaving, Stone moved briskly, getting Belle back to her stall. She seemed to know she was home, bobbing her head excitedly. Stone slipped off her saddle and took off the bit. "There you go, girl. You did good." He stroked her neck as she began eating from the manger.

"Did you like it?" A woman's voice carried through the barn along with footsteps.

"It was work, but kinda fun." Stone closed the stall door and stepped out, seeing Preston gliding toward him, talking to the woman walking next to him. "But my ass hurts something fierce."

Stone couldn't help himself. "It wouldn't if you wore proper jeans."

The wheels slowed and Preston rolled up to him. "I'll have you know that these jeans are Armani and cost more than anything you've ever worn in your life." The haughty tone carried through the barn.

"Is that so?" Stone glared down at him. "I guess girl's jeans are expensive," he retorted, suddenly enjoying picking on this guy. He needed to be taken down a peg or two, and he noticed that the woman with him, probably his mother, didn't come to his rescue. "No wonder your ass hurts—all those sparkles and crap must dig in good." Stone began walking away. "Not that I care, but a good old-fashioned pair of Wranglers work best for riding." Stone strode away and went to get his tools before returning. He still had stalls to clean, but he wanted to make sure Preston was gone before returning to work.

Kids came and went. He saw Eli walk through the barn and heard what he thought was a riding lesson. Stone continued working, listening to the sound of horsemen at work, until Eli approached him.

"There's a group therapy session in about half an hour. Can you help?"

"Sure." He was just finishing up the last stall.

"Good. You'll be working with Sherry. She's six, I believe, and doesn't talk much at all. Her father was killed a few months ago, and she hasn't spoken to anyone as far as we know. She seems to respond to the horses, though."

Stone stepped out of the now-clean stall, shutting the door behind him. "What do you want me to do?"

"Just walk the horse around the ring and talk to her. I just didn't want you to be surprised when she doesn't talk back."

Stone nodded his understanding and went to put away his tools. It had been a long day and he was tired. But the stalls were clean. As he walked to the tool closet, he could hear the sounds of laughter as people worked with their horses. "Damn it." He wiped his eyes. He missed Buster. He and the gelding had spent every day together, and it had practically broken his heart to leave him behind. He worried about him and hoped the old man was taking care of him. At least he knew Carl, his dad's hand, would most likely see to him.

Horses and happy voices filled the barn as students brought their mounts back to their stalls.

Eli and Joey followed them, getting horses ready for the therapy session. "Joey?"

Stone turned and saw Robbie at the barn door, but noticed that Joey was very busy. Closing the closet door, he rushed through the activity. "Joey's busy, but I'll help you."

"I can make it normally, but there's too much activity," Robbie explained as he took Stone's arm and they walked down the aisle, maneuvering together around the large beasts.

"Hey, Robbie." Stone released the man as Joey closed the stall door and slipped an arm around Robbie's waist.

"Thank you, Stone, for the help."

"You're welcome." Stone watched as Joey guided Robbie into the stall, and after Robbie mounted, Joey led the horse toward the ring. Once inside, Joey mounted as well, and they rode together with Robbie's hands around Joey's waist.

"Would you lead Mercury here to the ring and stay with him?" Eli asked. "I'll get Belle and we'll be ready. The kids will be here soon."

They arrived a few minutes later, but there was none of the laughter and cries of delight you'd expect from six-year-olds. "This is Sherry," her mother said gently, and Stone looked into the big, blue eyes of a small girl with golden hair, holding her mother's hand.

Eli bent down. "This is Mr. Stone. You can call him Stoney if you want. He's gonna help you with Mercury, okay?"

She looked through all of them and appeared to focus on the pony.

"I'll put you on the pony, honey." Her mother picked up and placed her on Mercury.

Stone got her feet set in the stirrups and then started leading her around the ring. "Have you ridden Mercury before?" Stone looked back and saw no reaction, but he did notice that she held on with one hand and was petting the pony with the other. "He's a nice horse, isn't he?" No answer. But she did look up and kept petting Mercury's neck. "Do you like horses? I do. I have one of my own back home, but I couldn't bring him here." No response at all. Stone kept walking and talking, trying another subject.

"Did your mom bring you?" Stone pointed and her gaze followed his hand. "She's very pretty." Big eyes traveled back to him. "You're pretty, too, just like your mom."

Stone saw tears stream down her face, but she kept stroking the horse as she looked at her mom and then back at Stone. "Daddy used to say that." Her voice was so soft.

She talked. Holy shit!!! Stone didn't know what to do, so he kept walking the pony. "What else did your daddy say?" No response. "Did he have a name for you? My mom used to call me Fidget because I couldn't sit still."

Her eyes got wide and then she smiled. "Daddy called me Ice Cream Girl."

Stone glanced around the ring as Eli and Joey walked their horses. Joey's had a small boy sitting in front, with Robbie holding him. All the riders were smiling. Stone continued walking and saw Joey lead his horse in before helping the little boy and then Robbie off the horse. Eli then led in his horse. After one final lap, Stone led Mercury toward the rail. After Stone tied off Mercury's lead, Sherry's mother walked by, but Sherry held out her arms to Stone and he lifted her off the pony, smiling when she put her arms around her neck.

"Did you have a nice ride, honey?"

Those big eyes looked at her mom and then at Stone before nodding. Stone put her down and she took her mother's hand. "We'll see the pony again next week." As they began to walk away, Sherry tugged her hand away and walked slowly to Stone before hugging his legs.

"Thank you, Stoney." She looked up at him, eyes bright and shining.

He patted her blonde hair lightly, and then she turned back to her mom, taking the shocked woman's hand. A tear ran down her cheek as she lifted her little girl off her feet, hugging her tight. "Thank you, whatever you did or said. Thank you." Her hand cradled the blonde head as she walked to the car. Stone walked on air as he finished the last of his chores and was still riding high as he walked toward the house for dinner.

Stone slipped off his boots and padded into the kitchen. Adelle smiled at him and handed him a warm mug. Geoff came in from the other room. "Could I talk to you?"

"Give the boy a minute, Mr. Geoff, he just got in," Adelle admonished lightly, and Geoff grinned back at her.

"Come to my office, then." Geoff turned and walked back through the doorway, shaking his head.

Stone couldn't help wondering what Geoff wanted, so he set the mug on the table and followed, figuring he'd better not tempt fate too much. He liked it here, but he'd sworn to himself he wouldn't get too comfortable. This could all end as fast as it started. Stone rapped lightly on the doorframe and stepped inside. It appeared that Geoff was already engrossed in something. "You wanted to see me?"

"Yeah." Geoff set down the papers, and Stone watched nervously, wondering.... "Sit down." Geoff didn't seem angry, which was good. "I heard what you did for Sherry. She and her mother stopped by before leaving, and the woman couldn't stop singing your praises."

"I just told her that her mother was pretty and that she was pretty, too, because she looked like her." Stone smiled.

Geoff looked confused. "The Biddles adopted Sherry when she was a baby. She isn't their biological daughter and doesn't look at all like her mother."

"That may be, but Sherry said her daddy used to say the same thing. In fact that was the first thing she said." Stone couldn't hide the pleasure that his innocent and accidental mistake had helped the little girl. But Stone's smile didn't last long as Geoff's expression changed.

"I also understand that you had a problem with another client."

Stone looked down at the floor. "Yes, sir." He was in for it now. No matter what happened back home, he always got blamed, and it was the same thing here. "I'll get my things and go." Stone stood up and walked out of the office, heading for the stairs. Maybe this was for the best. If he moved on, he wouldn't have a chance to miss this when they asked him to leave later.

"Stone." He heard Geoff's voice and turned, already halfway up the stairs. "Instead of jumping to conclusions, why don't you tell me about it."

Slowly, he walked back down the stairs, expecting to get hit as he stepped past Geoff and went back into the office. It surprised Stone when Geoff pulled up one of the other chairs and sat next to him. "Just tell me what happened."

Stone told Geoff the story, feeling stupid and ashamed. "I'm sorry I got mad at him, but he kept calling me 'Stable Boy' even after I told him my name. I shouldn't have said the things I did. I'm sorry."

"Yeah, well, he shouldn't have been baiting you, either." Stone waited for Geoff to tell him to leave or at least yell at him for costing the farm a client. "Go on upstairs and get cleaned up for dinner." Stone looked up from the floor, totally confused. "Stone, I offered you a job, and if I'm not happy, I'll tell you. You did great today with Sherry, and the barn hasn't looked that good in months." Stone stood up slowly. "And clients do not have the right to treat you the way he did today." Geoff stood up and went to his desk. "I'll call and tell him he doesn't need to come back."

Love Means ... Freedom

"No, please don't." Geoff was already dialing the phone. "I don't want you to lose a paying client over me."

Geoff slowly set down the phone. "We don't need clients like that. We don't mistreat anyone, and I won't let anyone on my farm be mistreated, either." Geoff eyes became hard.

Geoff wanted him and was willing to give up a paying client for him. Stone was stunned. No one wanted him. His father had tolerated him and used him as a workhorse after his mother had died. "I think we can help him. He may be a bit of an ass," Stone said, and Geoff's expression changed to a hint of a smile. "Okay, a lot of an ass," he amended, "but we can help him, and maybe that's more important." Stone couldn't hold back a smile.

Geoff sat down slowly, smiling right back. "Okay, but if he says anything to you, I want you to tell me or Joey. We'll throw him and his wheelchair out on his ear."

"Mr. Geoff and Mr. Stone, dinner is ready." Adelle's voice carried in from the kitchen.

Geoff walked around the desk. "Go get cleaned up."

Stone nodded and left the office before turning and heading up the stairs, hardly able to believe his luck. This had to be too good to be true. These people were just too damned nice. Reaching the top of the stairs, he stepped into the bathroom and closed the door. No one had been that nice to him, well, not since his mama, anyway. It was almost hard for him to understand. Looking in the mirror, he smiled. If Mr. Sparkly Jeans wanted to say something, let him go ahead. He'd put up with just about anything from that arrogant ass if it meant he could stay here—at least until they found out, and then no one would want him. Pushing the thought from his mind, Stone washed up and left the bathroom, bounding down the stairs and into the kitchen.

CHAPTER 4

PRESTON jumped at the knock on the front door. Parting the curtains, he peered out and saw Jasper standing on the front porch. "Come in." He'd just managed to get himself out of the wheelchair and comfortable on the sofa. At times like this, alone in the house, he felt both free and vulnerable at the same time—but he desperately wanted to be out of the chair for a little while, even though it meant leaving the front door unlocked. Preston turned down the television as he heard energetic stomping in the hall before his guest strode into the room. "I wasn't...." Preston's voice trailed off when he saw the expression on Jasper's face and he did a quick check, instantly trying to figure out what he'd done.

"What were you thinking? I work with those people, and you behaved like a complete and total ass!" Jasper stood next to the sofa glaring down at him, and if looks could kill, Preston knew he'd be shriveled to nothing in about three seconds. "They're some of the best people you will ever meet in your miserable, self-absorbed life, and you insulted one of them."

Preston felt his temper rising fast. "Who in hell are you talking about?"

Love Means ... Freedom

"Stable Boy. Does that ring a bell? You pompous ass." Jasper finally took a breath. "I can't believe you insulted the man who was trying to help you with your therapy."

"It was only some kid," Preston said weakly, trying to justify the unjustifiable. Jasper's body shook with rage and Preston backpedaled fast. "Hey, I'm sorry. I didn't know he was a friend of yours."

Jasper turned, leaning down, getting so close Preston could smell his breath as he pointed away. "I know Geoff and Eli because I work with them. They're some of the most giving people ever, and I've got a news flash for you, honey, you need them a hell of a lot more than they need you." Jasper stopped yelling and breathed regularly before shoving Preston's legs to the back of the sofa and sitting down. "They're one of the largest landowners in the county. Their land is measured in square miles. The therapy riding is something they do mainly for needy children. I asked them specifically if they could take you on, and you go and act like a big jerk."

"I'm sorry, okay. I didn't know his name and... fuck." Preston huffed, trying to figure out how he could save face. Usually he yelled louder and people backed down, but that didn't work with Jasper or Derrick. "I'm sorry, okay?" *What else could he say?*

"I wish you meant that."

That small phrase really hurt. Not because Jasper didn't believe him, but because he didn't believe it himself. He was never sorry for anything he did. The words were just a way to weasel out of it. "Look, Jasper, I don't know why I called him that, okay? I shouldn't have."

"No, you shouldn't have. And you are fucking lucky that kid is a hell of a lot nicer than you are." Preston released a huge breath; at least Jasper wasn't yelling at him anymore. "The only reason you're allowed back is because Stone, that's his name, by the way," Jasper said, glaring at him again, "thought they could help you and stopped Geoff from barring you from the place altogether."

Preston was taken aback. "He did that for me?"

"He sure as fuck did. I was able to get you an appointment on Thursday, and I'm going to take you so you don't insult someone else." Jasper got up and walked back toward the door. "I'll be here at noon, and you'd better be ready." Preston watched open-mouthed as Jasper left the room. "Oh, and by the way, if you ever want me to speak to you again, you better come up with an apology to end all apologies for Stone." Preston heard Jasper stomp out of the house, with the door closing hard enough to rattle the pictures.

Damn, he'd never seen Jasper so angry before, but he supposed he had a right to be. He'd treated Stone badly, really badly. He heard the door open and familiar footsteps in the hall. "Hey, Mom."

She walked into the living room as she took off her coat. "Was that Jasper I saw leaving?"

"Yeah."

"He looked angry." She hung up her coat and then walked back into the room.

"Mom, can I ask you something?" She sat in the chair across from him. "Have I treated you badly?"

She smiled. "Where did this come from?"

"Mom, I need to know."

"You've been through a lot since the accident." She dodged the question, and Preston had his answer as clearly as if she'd have just told him.

"Look, Mom, I'm sorry." She'd been as supportive as anyone could ask, and he could hear all the things he'd said to her over the last few months. He'd been short, rude, and downright mean to her and to everyone else. "I shouldn't have taken things out on you. It's not your fault I got hurt." It wasn't anyone's fault, except the driver, but he'd done his best to make the whole world pay. He began lifting himself and scooting closer to his chair, and she got up to help him. "Let me do it, Mom," he almost snapped, but caught himself. "I need to do this myself, but thank you." He saw her smile as she watched him use his legs to help maneuver his body into the chair.

"I have to make dinner." She got up, still smiling, and left the room.

"Can I help?" Preston called as he wheeled himself back toward the kitchen. He never helped around the house. His mom did it all, and maybe, just maybe, it was time he helped out. Maybe it was time he earned his keep.

"Of course." She looked at him skeptically, but went into the refrigerator and hauled things out, placing them on the table. "You could make the salad." She handed him a knife, and he went to work chopping vegetables and, when he was done, setting the table for the two of them. "Do you know how long it's since we did anything together?"

Preston stopped what he was doing and looked at her, thinking before shaking his head. She'd taken him everywhere he needed to go, but they hadn't done anything together, really together, in years. "Not really."

She didn't turn around, but he could hear her voice get slightly deeper. "You were about fifteen, and we went to the lake to visit my sister. You had more fun that week with your cousins." She kept her back to him, and Preston knew she was trying to keep from crying. "Helen didn't want her kids eating sugar, so we'd sneak off and get ice cream together."

Preston did remember that. When he thought about it, his mom had been pretty cool. "Has it been that long?" She nodded, and Preston thought back. After that summer, he'd gone on to high school, and his friends had been more important than his parents. After high school, he'd gone on to party away four years of college. Dad had paid the bills, and he'd done just enough to get by and keep from being cut off financially. Even after he'd graduated, he'd gotten a job he'd absolutely hated, but he couldn't keep it after the accident. "When you were younger, what did you do for fun?"

His mom turned around, smiling. "I sang in the choir, and your father and I used to go camping when we were first married." She wiped her hands on her apron absently. "That was before we had you and his career took off." The wistful look on her face faded. "Then I took care of the house and raised you." The timbre of her voice shifted—Preston hated that sound. He'd heard it before, whenever she remembered that he was grown and wouldn't need her anymore.

"I was thinking," Preston said as he brightened his voice, "if you'll drive, why don't we go see a movie after dinner, just the two of us?"

The look of surprise and delight on her face warmed his heart. He had indeed been a complete shit to her and to everyone else. All she wanted was a little of his time and attention, just like he'd wanted from her when he was growing up. "I'd like that." She began bringing dishes to the table, and the two of them sat down to eat, their usual quiet table replaced with laughter and a happy banter he'd never thought he could have with her. Yeah, his mom was pretty special.

PRESTON was in the car with Jasper, and his friend hadn't said a thing since they'd left the house. "Come on, Jas, you can't stay mad at me forever." He turned toward his friend and batted his eyes at him. Jasper tried but failed to suppress a smile.

"You shit." He batted his hand at him as they approached the farm.

"I know, but you love me." He kept up the harmless flirting until they pulled into the driveway and up to the barn. Jasper pulled out the hated wheelchair, and Preston maneuvered himself into it. "I'll be so happy when I can burn this thing," he grumbled as he wheeled himself away from the car and through the packed snow into the barn.

Love Means ... *Freedom*

Huge, majestic heads peeked out of stalls and watched as he glided down the aisle and then out through the passage into the indoor riding arena. He saw Joey and Stable Boy. He suppressed the thought—Stone, his name was Stone. "Hey, guys." He put on his best smile and wheeled himself over to where they were standing. "Are you ready for me?"

He saw Stone nod his head to Joey and then walk back toward the barn. "Sorry." Joey got closer. "We got a little behind, but Stone will be right back with Belle."

Preston's first instinct was impatience, and he worked to push it away. It probably wasn't their fault, and it wasn't as though he had some pressing appointment, so he sat back and relaxed. "No problem." He smiled up at Joey and watched as the person in the ring finished up his ride. "Who is that?" The man looked like he'd spent his whole life on a horse.

Joey smiled. "That's Eli. He and Geoff own the farm."

Preston let his attention focus on the handsome man and the sleek black horse he was riding. The man was beautiful, and Preston watched his lithe form maneuver the horse with masterful precision. "It looks like they were made for each other," Preston commented, as a jolt of desire shot through him.

"He won't let anyone but Geoff or Eli ride him." Joey turned to look at him. "Thunder's a stallion and tends to be a little aggressive. Most farms only use them for breeding, but that horse would do anything for them. I think he's grateful he's still got all his bits." Joey laughed and Preston joined in as Eli pulled the horse to a stop and dismounted, leading him out of the ring and waving as he disappeared into the passage.

The younger man appeared leading Belle, the horse Preston had ridden the last time, slowly walking her to the base of the ramp. "We're going to try a little more activity this time. I want you to use your legs as much as you can. I know you can grip the horse but can't stand yet, and that's fine. We'll ride a little longer today, and if you're comfortable, you can even steer," Joey instructed.

"You mean like really ride?" Preston wheeled himself up the ramp with Joey following.

"Sure, that's the whole idea. Teach you to ride. It takes longer because of your legs, but you can learn if you're patient and willing to spend the time."

With Joey's help, Preston shifted himself onto the horse, and after getting help putting his feet in the stirrups, Stone led the horse on their slow walk around the ring. Preston kept his legs tightened around the horse, and he could feel the animal's power beneath him. "Could we please go a little faster?" Preston made a point of asking nicely.

Stone turned and looked up at him. "You'll have to ask Joey. I'm just the stable boy, remember?" The kid looked so hurt, and Preston looked, really looked at him for the first time. His hair was long and wavy, flopping into his big expressive eyes. The kid was attractive, and that vulnerable look he had made him even cuter.

"I'm sorry about that. I should never have called you that." Preston kept watching Stone as they continued around the ring.

"Yeah, okay." Stone turned around and Preston felt let down, like he wanted Stone looking at him.

"I mean it. I should never have treated you that way. Here you're trying to help me walk again, and I acted like an ass." It was suddenly important that Stone forgive him. Maybe it was because he had the face of an angel, but Stone's opinion of him suddenly mattered.

"Thanks." Stone looked at him again, and he felt a funny fluttering in his stomach and an urge to do anything he could think of to keep that gaze on him. "I shouldn't have said what I said, either." Stone's eyes flashed up at him for a few seconds and then returned to the task at hand. He also started walking faster.

Stone turned around again. "Let your body move with the horse. Use your legs to keep yourself steady and let your body flow with her movement."

Preston followed Stone's advice, and the ride became much easier and a great deal more pleasant.

"That's it," he heard Joey call from the other side of the ring. "You're doing great." They continued walking, and Joey motioned them over. "Hand him the reins and we'll show him how to steer."

Stone placed the leather loop over the horse's head and handed it to Preston. "Like this." Stone took Preston's hands and showed him how to hold the reins, their skin touching, and he felt a small shiver run through him. "That's better. If you want to change direction, all you need to do is lay the reins against her neck in the direction you want to turn. I'll be right here with you."

Preston was almost shaking with nervous excitement. "Okay. Um, how do I make her go?"

"Just nudge her side with your foot and click your tongue."

Preston wasn't sure he had the strength in his legs yet, but gave it a try, clicking his tongue and kicking slightly. To his surprise, the horse began walking forward and started traveling around the ring. He was riding, actually riding, a horse. Preston could hardly believe it. After the accident, he'd figured things like this wouldn't be a possibility. The doctors hadn't been hopeful he'd ever be able to move his legs again, let alone walk, and here he was riding a horse. Granted, his legs weren't strong enough for him to walk yet, but it was happening.

Looking around, he saw Stone standing in the center of the ring, watching him intently. Preston wanted to think he was looking at him, but he figured he was just doing his job. "Why don't you turn to the left and walk her straight across the ring." Stone's soft voice carried straight to Preston's ear. "She's used to walking around the ring, and I want her to know that you're the one in control."

"Okay, I'll try." Preston rested the reins on her neck, and she looked that way and eventually began to turn. Preston picked up the reins, and she immediately went back to her old path around the edge of the ring.

"Try it again and tug slightly." Preston did as instructed, and this time Belle turned and began walking across the ring. "Excellent. When you come to the other side, have her go halfway around the ring in the opposite direction from before and then cross the ring again."

"Okay." Preston found himself smiling as he sat tall and rested the reins against the right side of Belle's neck. She turned again and began walking around the ring. Partway around the ring, he turned her again, and they walked across the ring.

"That's great. See how she responds to you?" Stone walked closer, smiling brightly up at him, and Preston returned the grin, looking into those hair-shaded eyes, and he felt his body respond in a big way. Damn, his face lit up when he smiled. "What you did was show her that you were in control. Do that and she'll do what you want."

"Is it always that easy?"

Stone laughed, and Preston felt himself jerk in his pants as that fluttery feeling increased. "God no! Belle's used to novices and has a great manner. With some horses, it's a constant battle, but for advanced riders, the challenge is to build the trust and respect needed to work together."

"How are your legs feeling?" Joey's voice cut across the ring.

Preston turned toward him and pulled back on the reins, stopping Belle. "Good."

"Do they feel tight?"

He saw a smaller man carefully make his way toward Joey and saw him slide an arm around the newcomer's waist. "A little, but in a good way."

Love Means ... Freedom

"Okay. Another fifteen minutes should be enough for today," Joey said as Jasper joined the two men near the rail, and Preston started Belle walking again. He noticed the men talking whenever he passed by and sometimes wondered what they were talking about, but Stone kept him occupied until the session ended, and then they helped him back in his chair.

"That was great." Preston said, smiling. "Thanks, Stone."

"You're welcome." Stone smiled back briefly and then walked away, leading Belle back toward the barn.

"Preston." Jasper's voice brought his attention back to what was happening. "This is Joey's partner, Robbie. Robbie Jameson, this is Preston Harding."

Robbie held out his hand and waited, his attention off somewhere else. "Pleased to meet you."

Preston took the hand, and Robbie's face turned toward his. "Good to meet you too."

"Are you going to continue with the sessions?"

"I'd like to, if you have time available."

Joey and Jasper conferred and agreed that two half-hour sessions a week would be good to start. They made the appointments and, after saying their good-byes, Preston wheeled himself through the passage and out into the barn. He saw Stone working and stopped. "Thanks again, Stone." The working man waved, and Preston continued on to the car.

"So I take it this session was better than the last," Jasper commented as he closed his door.

"Yeah." He sat quietly, thinking of a young man in a tight pair of blue jeans that hugged a pair of legs and showed off the tightest butt he'd seen in a long time.

Jasper began to laugh. "See, I told you."

"What?" He grinned across at his friend.

41

"See, I told you that you just might meet someone with brains." Jasper put the car in gear.

"I believe you said someone with more than air between his ears," Preston clarified with a chuckle.

"I believe I did, and if I'm not mistaken, that young man you couldn't take your eyes off of the entire time you were here just proves my point."

"I was just paying attention during the therapy session." He crossed his arms across his chest, his smile turning to a scowl.

"You should pay that kind of attention during our sessions." Preston saw Jasper's expression as he drove, eyes gleaming with mischief. "You don't need to get all huffy—he was looking at you the same way," Jasper teased, as they bounced over one of the country hills.

"No, he wasn't," Preston protested, but he couldn't help feeling a little flip of excitement at the thought. "He was just doing his job."

Jasper looked over at him and then turned his attention to the road. "If you say so."

Love Means ... *Freedom*

CHAPTER 5

STONE heard voices in the house and rushed down the stairs, coming to a halt at the tables that filled the living room. "Hey, Eli, can I help?"

"Sure, the folding chairs are in the basement at the base of the stairs."

He looked around the room. "Where's Adelle?"

Eli's eyes danced. "Fridays are her day off. After the first week, she pronounced that her job didn't entail feeding every man under creation and most certainly didn't mean she should clean up after them. We agreed, so for tonight we're on our own."

"Where is she?"

Eli shrugged. "Geoff gives her use of one of the cars for the day, but no one's had the guts to ask her where she goes."

Stone hurried to the door and made his way into the dank area under the house, finding the chairs right where Eli said they were. Grabbing two in each hand, he made his way up the stairs and back into the living room. "Should I set these up?" Eli nodded and handed him a cloth. Stone wiped off the chairs and set them around the table. "What's all this for anyway?"

"Tonight's Geoff's poker night." He placed bowls of chips on the tables. "From what I understand, Len, Geoff's dad, and Geoff's father, Cliff, started the tradition years ago, and Geoff has carried it on."

"Do you play too?"

Eli shook his head. "Geoff has tried to teach me, but I'm awful, so I usually sit and watch. Sometimes Robbie and I go somewhere together and let the boys have their fun." Eli continued the preparations, and Stone got the last of the chairs from the basement, setting them around the tables as the back door opened and closed. "Stone," he heard Eli calling, and went into the kitchen. "This is Len, Geoff's dad, and his partner Chris."

They held out their hands, and Stone shook them, introducing himself.

"So, you're the young man Geoff has been telling me about?" Len asked, releasing his hand.

Stone colored slightly. "I guess so."

Len smiled. "Don't be shy. Geoff has been telling me good things."

The back door opened and banged closed again. Boots stomped before more people entered the room. "Hey, Eli." Geoff hugged his partner, stealing a soft kiss before turning to the other people in the room. "Look who I found."

Stone smiled as he saw Jasper walk into the kitchen. He knew he had a slight crush on the man, who immediately approached and hugged him hello before greeting everyone else. "Derrick will be right in. He had to get something from the car."

Stone knew that Jasper was off limits, and he even liked Derrick, but this was the first person, except maybe Geoff, whom he felt he could talk to about who he was. He and Jasper had spent a few hours over the past week talking when Jasper would stop by to check on Preston's progress. "Do you play poker?" Stone asked. It seemed to him that Jasper could do everything.

Love Means ... Freedom

Geoff answered the question. "Hell, yes. Last week he went home with all my money."

"Have you ever played?" Jasper asked, and Stone shook his head. His father would never allow cards in the house. "Tools of the devil," he used to call them. Never mind that the man used to drink like a fish and would hit him for the slightest infraction—but anything fun was inherently evil. "I'll teach you if you want."

Stone smiled. "Thanks."

"Is there anything we can do to help?" Derrick offered, carrying his dishes to the counter. "I know we came early, but you always do all the work." Stone watched as Derrick and Eli finished up their preparations, talking together. Stone was about to ask Jasper to explain poker to him when a cell phone rang. Jasper reached into his pocket, checking the display before answering.

"Preston, what's going on?" Stone leaned against the counter, waiting for Jasper. "You've got to be kidding. You've told him you're gay, right?" Stone wondered what was happening as he heard concern creep into Jasper's voice. "When's this supposed to happen?" Jasper checked his watch. "I'm at Geoff and Eli's. It's poker night." Jasper listened again. "No, I don't think they'll mind if you hang out for a while." Jasper looked over at Geoff, who nodded, and Stone felt an unfamiliar clench in his stomach. Preston was coming over here? Since Preston's last therapy session a few days ago, Stone had found himself wondering what the man would look like out of his chair—and out of his clothes, if the truth be told. But he was more than a little nervous around him. Preston had apologized for being mean to him, but he wasn't too sure he really wanted to spend too much time around him. If he was honest, he was a little afraid of him, but he could barely admit that to himself, and sure as hell wasn't about to tell anyone else that.

"I'll be there in a few minutes." Jasper hung up the phone. "I need to rescue Preston." He turned to Geoff. "Do you mind if he joins us? I know he's been a pain, but he's not really a bad guy."

Geoff looked at Stone and then back at Jasper. "As long as he behaves himself."

"I need to go pick him up; I'll be back as soon as I can." Jasper retrieved his coat. "Would you come with me?"

At first Stone looked around before realizing Jasper was talking to him. "If you need my help, sure."

"Sometimes Preston has difficulty getting in and out of my truck, and I'd appreciate your help."

"Okay, I'll be right back." Stone got his coat and returned to see Derrick giving Jasper a gentle kiss. Stone followed Jasper to his truck, and they headed out of the drive and down the country roads toward town.

"Is that where Preston lives?" Stone remarked as they pulled into the long drive of what Stone thought was the biggest house he'd ever seen.

"Yeah."

Stone looked at Jasper. "Then why's he so mean sometimes? If I lived in a place like this, I'd think I died and went to Heaven. Growing up, our farmhouse was only four small rooms. This place looks like a castle or something."

"Stone," Jasper said as he pulled up and parked by the garage, "just because someone lives in a big house and has money doesn't mean they're happy."

"I know that, but it's gotta help, right?" Stone actually smiled as he peered out the window at the massive house.

Jasper chuckled. "Come on, let's go rescue Preston." Opening the door, Jasper climbed out and Stone followed, walking up to the front door and ringing the bell. Stone looked around at all the shrubs and bushes pruned into balls and cones, each one perfectly shaped and lit with white Christmas lights.

Love Means ... Freedom

The door opened slowly. "Jasper, we weren't expecting you." Preston's mother smiled at them as she stepped back and opened the door.

"Thank God you're here." Preston rolled toward them as they entered. "He's driving me crazy."

"Preston, he's your father and only wants what's best for you," she soothed as she closed the door.

"No, he doesn't, Mom. He wants what's best for him and his precious reputation. A gay son just doesn't fit in with his world view." Preston opened the closet near the door and pulled his coat off a hanger. "Let's get out of here while he's still on the phone."

"Preston, you can't leave. Your father invited someone to dinner for you to meet."

"That's why I'm leaving, Mom." Preston shrugged on his coat.

"Where do you think you're going?" Stone turned toward the sound of the booming voice and saw a large man who had to be Preston's father. "You're expected for dinner, and I have someone you're going to meet."

Preston turned toward his father, glaring at him. "No, I'm not, Dad. I'm tired of you shoving these air-headed, big-boobed bimbos at me. I'm gay and it's not going to change."

"Bullshit. You just haven't met the right woman yet."

Stone found himself rolling his eyes in sympathy. That sounded so much like his own father, except his father had punctuated his point by slapping Stone on the head until he saw stars. Stone's initial reaction was to back away from Preston's father just like he'd backed away from his own. Then he stepped forward and leaned down to Preston, saying, "No big-boobed bimbo is going to take you away from me!" Without thinking further, he leaned down and slammed his lips against Preston's. At first, Preston stiffened and tried to pull away, but Stone kept kissing and then felt those firm, hot lips part slightly. For a second,

47

he forgot he was standing in Preston's house with both his parents looking on and just went with the feel and taste of Preston's lips against his. A hand on his shoulder pulled Stone back to reality, and he pulled away. Stone looked at Preston and saw his eyes widen, both of them breathing hard.

Preston was the first to recover. "Let's go."

Stone glanced away from Preston and saw the shocked look on his parents' faces. Jasper helped Preston out of the door and down the few steps to the sidewalk. Once on the concrete, they moved quickly, and soon Preston was in the truck between Stone and Jasper. Doors closed, and they pulled out and down the driveway. As soon as they reached the road, all three of them broke into fits of laughter, with Preston resting against Stone's shoulder, laughing the hardest.

"Why did you do that?" He was still laughing, but the mirth had begun to die away.

"I figured if he saw you kiss another guy, he might actually believe you were gay." That might have been why he'd done it, but Stone could still feel the tingle of Preston's lips against his. "I think he got the point." Maybe Preston was mad at him and he shouldn't have done it; it had been a gut reaction, and his rashness had gotten him into trouble before.

"No kidding, I don't think I can ever remember my father being stunned speechless before." They all settled down, and Stone felt Preston bump their shoulders together. "Thank you."

"For what? Kissing you? It was no problem." Stone felt shy and looked out the window. He'd liked the kiss, it was pretty incredible, but he was sure it didn't mean anything, at least to Preston. He'd done it on a whim, but when he was kissing Preston, he felt something. His body had reacted and he'd felt himself get hard as a rock. Jasper and Preston started talking about something that filled the space, and Stone gazed out the window, hypersensitive to everywhere that Preston's body touched his. And after what seemed like a split second, Jasper pulled the truck into the drive at the farm.

Love Means ... Freedom

The truck stopped, and Stone slid out, letting Preston scoot over. Carefully, Stone pulled the wheelchair out of the truck bed, assembled it, and held it steady while Jasper helped Preston as he shifted into it. A phone began to ring, and Preston shifted in his chair. Digging for it, he checked the display and shoved it back in his pocket. "He'll never leave me alone." The phone stopped ringing, and Stone began maneuvering the chair through the snow toward the back door as Preston reached for the phone again. "No more calls tonight," he said, and the phone chirped as it was shut down.

"Won't your dad get mad at you?" Stone asked as he walked backward, dragging the chair to the steps. If he'd done something like that to his father, there'd be hell to pay.

"Probably, but I can't stand it anymore. He just has to face reality."

Stone tilted the chair back and maneuvered Preston into the house while Jasper held the door. Coats were slipped off and snow stamped off boots and wiped off wheels before they entered the kitchen.

The house was filled with voices and laughter. Jasper walked toward the living room with Preston gliding behind him and Stone bringing up the rear. "Hey, guys, you remember Jasper," Geoff's voice boomed above the din. "And this is Stone, and the guy with his own seat is Preston." Greetings were exchanged all around, and room was made at the tables for the three of them.

"I've never played before." Stone didn't quite know what to do.

"No problem." Geoff sat down next to him. "Just watch for tonight, and next week you can join in if you want to."

Stone took a seat, and Preston wheeled himself up next to him. "Have you played before?" Lumpy, one of the farm hands, asked as he shuffled the cards.

"Sure, deal me in." Stone watched as Preston passed over some money.

"The game's seven-card stud, so ante up and let's see if I can win my money back." Lumpy began dealing, and Stone watched until Preston, of all people, leaned toward him and showed him his cards. Stone moved closer and couldn't help inhaling the man's clean, earthy scent.

"The trick is to not let any sort of expression cross your face, so the other players don't know what kind of hand you have."

Stone saw that Preston had a little of everything and watched him bet before more cards were dealt. He wasn't sure what Preston was doing, but watched closely as more cards were turned over. He had no idea what all the words meant, but appreciated that Preston kept explaining the terms as they went along. "We'll bet twenty." They were playing for dimes, but they were serious enough that you'd have thought big money was at stake.

Stone watched as a number of guys folded their hands. He tried to keep his expression level even as he wondered what Preston was doing. As far as he could tell, the man had nothing.

"Call," Geoff answered and threw in some chips. More cards were dealt, and again Preston bet. Stone saw Geoff's confidence begin to waver just a little; then he threw in his cards, and Preston pulled the money toward him with a big smile. "What'd you have?"

"Gotta pay to see 'em." Preston smiled up at him and Stone smiled back, and the cards passed to the next person. Preston leaned to Stone and whispered softly in his ear, "That was a bluff." Stone nodded and felt a tingle up his back as Preston went back to playing.

As the evening wore on, they played and laughed as the pile of chips in front of Preston grew larger. "Stone's gonna take this hand for me."

"Are you sure?" Excitement warred with nervousness as the cards were dealt to him and he picked up a pair of sevens. That seemed to be good, and when another one appeared face up in front of him, he had to keep himself from smiling. He placed a small bet and it got raised. He called, and more cards were dealt. He bet again and a few people

Love Means ... Freedom

dropped out, but Geoff and Joey stayed in. Geoff raised him, and he began to get nervous. Preston had backed away from the table and wasn't looking at the cards. "Do what your gut tells you."

Stone raised the bet, and both Geoff and Joey called. "Three sevens." Stone grinned as Joey threw in his cards.

"Sorry." Geoff set down a pair of nines to go with the one he had showing.

"Wait, Stone." Preston pointed to the table. "You have a full house, sevens and tens."

Geoff smiled. "Yes, you do," he said, and he pushed the pot toward him.

Stone beamed and added the chips to Preston's pile, but Preston stopped him. "This is your first pot—that's yours." Stone grinned, eyes crinkling, and stacked the chips in front of him. He knew it was dumb luck, but everyone made him feel so good, like he belonged, especially Preston. This was so different and completely unexpected. Stone didn't win the next hand, but the evening broke up soon after and he made a few dollars with his winnings.

The guys helped clean up and began to say their good-nights. "Thanks, Preston. That was really nice of you," Stone said as Preston followed Jasper. "No problem," Preston called as Stone found himself at the table alone. He got up and began folding down the chairs, getting them ready to take to the basement. He noticed that Jasper and Preston were whispering back and forth. "This isn't high school, Preston," Jasper said, and then he left the room.

"Is something wrong? Is Jasper mad?"

"No, he's just reminding me to be a man."

Stone tucked two chairs under each arm. "What about?"

"I wanted him to talk to someone for me and he told me to do it myself."

"Oh." Stone took the chairs through the house and into the basement, and then returned to the room, where Preston appeared to be waiting for him expectantly. Not knowing what was happening, he began folding up more chairs until he felt a hand on his arm, and he jumped, almost dropping the chair.

"I wanted to ask you something." Stone noticed Preston squirming in his chair.

"Okay." Stone stopped moving, wondering if he'd done something wrong. Instinctively, he began fidgeting and reached for the chairs.

"Stone." Preston touched his arm again. "I was wondering if you'd be willing to go out with me?" A crash made them both jump, and Stone realized he'd let go of the chair he was holding.

"Sorry." Embarrassed, he felt himself color as he scrambled to pick up the chair and set it against the table. "You mean like a date? Why?"

"Yes, like a date." Preston smiled at him, but Stone could feel his stomach clenching.

"But why?"

Stone felt Preston's hand against his. "Because I acted like an ass and I want to make it up to you." Stone didn't know what to say, but he saw Preston color, and the man actually looked shy, which he didn't think happened very often. "And because of that kiss."

Stone touched his lips on reflex, remembering the kiss as well. "Okay." He could hardly believe he was agreeing to this, and as soon as he'd agreed, he began to wonder what he'd gotten himself in for.

CHAPTER 6

"So, DID your father flip out when you got home?" Jasper asked.

Preston held the phone beneath his chin as he moved around the room, trying to figure out what he should wear on his date with Stone. "No. In fact, he's been unusually silent over the last few days. So either he's plotting a creative demise for me or he's decided if he ignores it, my gayness will just go away." He wheeled himself to the closet and began sorting through his shirts.

"You don't seem upset about it."

Preston sighed as he continued looking. He'd stopped worrying about what his father thought years ago. If he didn't care, then the man couldn't hurt him, and Lord knew his father had hurt him plenty over the years. "Nothing to be upset about; it's quiet and I'm happy." *At least for now.*

"So what time's your date?"

"He's picking me up in about an hour." Preston couldn't drive, but to his gratitude, Stone had said that Geoff would loan him a car.

He heard Jasper laugh. "Thank God. Can you imagine having to ask your mother for a ride?" Peals of laughter rang through the receiver as Preston almost dropped the phone.

"You know, since the accident, there have been a number of things that I've cringed over. Having to go to the bathroom with someone's help, being dressed, and getting a sponge bath from a complete stranger who was so hairy I thought I was being bathed by Cousin It, but I draw the line at taking my mother on a date." He started laughing, and Jasper's giggles started up again.

"Hey, I'm sorry, but Derrick just got home." Preston heard a door close behind Jasper, followed by a completely different type of giggle. "I'll see you tomorrow for our therapy session, and you can tell me everything." Jasper hung up as his giggles got deeper.

Closing the phone, Preston found the shirt he was looking for and began to change. It took him some time, but he was able to dress and clean up on his own. All set, he wheeled himself out of the room and got his coat, waiting near the front door for Stone to arrive.

"You're really going out with that boy?"

Preston turned around and sighed. He'd hoped he would be able to leave without seeing his father. "Yes, Dad."

He sipped his Scotch and looked thoughtful. "The one who kissed you?"

"Yes." Preston smiled when he saw a slight shudder travel through his father. The first chink in the man's formidable armor and the look on his face made Preston stop and look for a second. He hadn't seen that look in a long time, and it gave him hope. He waited to see what his father would do next, but the man just stood there, looking at him. "Look, Dad." He sighed and wheeled himself closer. "I'm gay. I've never liked girls that way and I never will." He actually seemed to be listening. "I like men and that's not going to change, even if you parade the Dallas Cowboy Cheerleaders through the living room naked." He smiled and saw what he hoped was a ghost of a smile on his father's face. For the first time, Preston thought he might be getting

54

Love Means ... Freedom

through. Hell, this was the longest conversation they'd had in a long time, even if it was rather one-sided. "I'm sorry you're disappointed, but as you like to say, 'facts are facts'." Preston waited for some sort of reaction from the man, hoping for anything, but all he did was shake his head and walk down the hall, a door closing a few seconds later.

"Damn," Preston whispered, as he blinked away the wetness that threatened to spill from his eyes. He refused to cry over him. He'd already done enough of that and he wasn't going to do it any more. He knew he'd never been the son his father had wanted. Preston spent much of his teenage years trying to get his father's attention and approval, but by the time he graduated high school, he'd found that was impossible. Whatever he did just wasn't good enough. "I know you wanted a football star, but you got me instead." He turned and looked at where his father had disappeared. "Fuck," he said as he wiped his eyes again. "No wonder I act like an ass all the time." The one thing he wanted, he could never have. He had to accept that his father would never accept a gay son.

The doorbell rang, and Preston dabbed his eyes and wheeled himself to the door, opening it. Stone stood on the doorstep, looking around, as twitchy as a cat, his lower lip between his teeth, nervously chewing. He looked adorably attractive as he shifted his weight from one leg to the other. Preston smiled and glided back. "Come in."

Stone gingerly stepped over the threshold, looking around the room. "I can't get over how rich you are." Stone's eyes were wide as saucers.

"I'm not; my father is. I just live here." That was as good a way to describe it as any. This house hadn't felt like a home in a very long time. His mother was great, and things were good when his father was gone, but the minute he returned, it was as if the snow from the outside moved inside as well.

"I just live at the farm too." Stone's words and tone shocked Preston. Looking into his face, he saw his feelings echoed back to him.

"Not that Geoff and Eli haven't been nice to me and made me feel welcome."

Preston went to the coat closet and pulled a coat off a hanger. "I know. You just don't feel as though it's your home." He began maneuvering the coat over his shoulders. "This building hasn't felt like home in a long time." Preston's arm got caught in his coat sleeve, and he felt Stone's hand on him, the warmth going right through his shirt, guiding his arm into the sleeve. Finally, he had the coat on. "Thank you. Shall we go?" He needed to get out of here. The place was becoming so oppressive, and he didn't want to feel that way. He wanted to enjoy Stone's company. This was a date, after all.

Stone led the way, and Preston followed him outside and down the walk to the car. It took him a few minutes to get out of his chair and into the strange vehicle, but he managed. Stone folded his chair and stood it on the floor of the back seat.

Preston smiled. "I made reservations for us at the Harborside Country Club."

Stone closed his door and started the car, a look of concern on his face. "Am I dressed well enough for a place like that?"

"You look wonderful." He really did. The color of his shirt showed off his wonderful, deep eyes, and his pants hugged his thighs. "I wanted to take you there to show you that I'm truly sorry for how I treated you."

"Is that why you really asked me out?"

"No, I asked you out because I want to get to know you. I was mean to you and you stuck up for me anyway." Stone looked over at him, confused. "Jasper told me the only reason I was allowed back for riding therapy was because of you. No one's ever done anything like that for me before." There was so much more to it, but he was having a tough time putting it into words. "Let me just say that I asked you out because I like you, and I hope that you can forgive me and maybe get to like me too." Preston felt all fluttery and weird. He'd never thought or cared what others thought of him, but Stone had broken through his defenses, and he found himself in uncharted territory.

Stone's smile made his nervousness subside and the flutters in his stomach jump off the scale. "Can you give me directions?"

"Sure." Preston returned Stone's smile. "Go back toward town and I'll tell you where to turn." Stone drove and Preston guided them to the country club entrance and into one of the member parking spaces near the door.

It took some maneuvering, but he got himself into the hated chair, through the door, and into the restaurant without much assistance. Stone did help a little. Preston hated that he needed help to get around, but Stone's assistance didn't seem to bother him, particularly since Stone would touch him lightly whenever he helped. "I have a reservation for Harding," Preston told the hostess, and she led them to a table near the huge windows that looked out on a grove of trees lit with floodlights. She removed a chair, and Preston positioned himself at the table, with Stone sitting across from him. She handed them both menus and then left.

Preston watched Stone open his menu and thought his eyes would bug out of his head. "Is this right?"

Preston smiled. "Yes. Don't worry; order whatever you'd like. The food's the best in town." He worried that maybe he should have chosen a different place. He hadn't thought about how Stone would react, and he didn't want him to feel uncomfortable. He'd only wanted to take him somewhere special.

Stone nodded and Preston watched with a smile as Stone gawked over the menu. "What are escargot?" He pronounced it "*s-car-gott.*"

"They're snails in garlic butter." Stone pulled a face, and Preston began to chuckle. "Don't worry, I don't like them, either. Too chewy. I suggest the steak *frites*—best french fries you'll ever have. They serve them with mayonnaise, and they're unbelievable." The waitress came by, and Stone ordered a soda. Preston would normally order a beer, but he figured that Stone was too young, so he ordered a soda as well. When she returned, they placed their orders and were left alone again. "Are you from around here?"

"No. I was raised outside Petoskey, on a small farm."

"How long have you been here?"

"Little over a week." Stone began to squirm in his chair.

"Do you like it at the farm?" Preston noticed that Stone stopped moving and smiled across the table at him.

"Yeah. They're all really good to me." The server brought their meals, placing a plate in front of each of them. "This looks really good." Stone leaned forward, inhaling deeply before starting to eat.

The food was great, and they smiled across the table at one another. Preston tried a few times to start a conversation, but he wasn't sure where to go. "What do you like to do for fun?"

For the first time that evening, Preston saw Stone's face light up. "I used to love spending time with Buster, my horse." Stone's smile faded slowly.

"Stone, what happened?" Preston hated asking, but the sadness on that face was too much for him to take. Without thinking, Preston reached across the table, touching Stone's fingers lightly. "I'll listen if you want to talk." He smiled inside when he realized he was taking a page from Jasper's playbook, and that he really wanted to be there for Stone. Stone's eyes got wide, and Preston could feel the gaze probing him, like he was trying to make up his mind.

"My father threw me out a few months ago, and I've been moving around."

"Because you're gay?" Preston asked, and Stone nodded.

"Life with my dad was always tough, but it got worse after my mother died. I think at some point he stopped looking at me like his kid and started looking at me like a farmhand he didn't have to pay." Stone put down his fork and took a gulp of water. "I don't know why I did it, but I told him I thought I was gay. He beat me until I could barely breathe and then threw me out of the house." Stone gulped and took another drink of water, and then, to Preston's surprise, he continued. "I worked here and there for a while and managed to save a little. Then I tried heading south, but...." There was that look again. "I only made it this far and the guy I was riding with threw me out."

Preston knew there was more to the story by the way Stone refused to meet his eyes. "It's okay. You don't have to tell me anything you're not comfortable with."

"The worst thing is that I had to leave Buster behind. I can take care of myself, but he can't." Stone's voice caught in his throat. "I don't even know if...."

Preston gripped Stone's hand, letting him know he was there for him. "I'm sorry."

"Me too." Stone wiped his eyes. "I'm messing up our dinner."

"We could talk about something more pleasant, like the joys of physical therapy." To Preston's relief, Stone smiled, the mood lightened, and they started to talk. Stone's story had really broken the ice, and Preston told him what it was like growing up in the Harding household.

"Sounds like we have a lot in common." Stone said between bites.

Preston swallowed his french fry. "Yeah, I guess we do. We both just wanted our father's love, and neither of us got it." Preston fished out another fry. "I think we need to find something happier to talk about, or this is going to go down as the most depressing first date in history."

Stone looked up, smiling, and Preston felt Stone's hand slide against his. "We could return to the joys of therapy." Stone's wicked smile started Preston laughing, and Stone joined him. "Aren't we both a barrel of laughs?"

"Doesn't really matter, I'm having a good time." Preston snuck a look at Stone and smiled a little when he heard him say he was too.

God, he felt like he was back in high school, except then he'd never had the guts to tell anyone about himself. He just hid behind a wall of arrogance.

They finished their meal, the conversation full of laughter and smiles. It felt so good to see Stone smile and to know he was smiling at him and because of him. He even thought he saw him relax a few times.

"Would you like any dessert?" He hadn't heard their server approach, his conversation with Stone capturing his full attention. They were both full and declined dessert, and after paying the check, Preston got his coat and allowed Stone to guide him through the now-crowded dining room and out to the car.

"Thank you, Stone," Preston said as he got into the car.

"You're welcome." Stone collapsed the chair and stored it in the back before getting in and closing the door.

"Stone." Preston leaned closer, the seat creaking slightly. "Thank you."

"For what?" Stone didn't stop him as he slid a hand behind his neck, the skin warm and smooth.

"For confiding in me. No one's ever done that before." Preston tugged gently, and Stone moved closer, his lips so close he could feel their warmth tantalizing him.

"Maybe you've never listened before." Stone's lips touched his ever so softly in return, and Preston found his heart pounding as he opened his mouth slightly and touched Stone's soft, sweet lips, and he heard a soft sound from deep in Stone's throat—a soft, sort of mewling sound that went right to Preston's core and made his beating heart sing. After months of seeing each other and sleeping together, Kent had never given him the flutters and tingles that Stone's tender, simple kiss did.

The sound of a car behind them pulled them back to the here and now, and they both realized they were still sitting in the restaurant parking lot. Preston felt Stone pull away and saw his finger touch his lips. That simple gesture told him that Stone had felt the same thing he had. With a glance and a smile back at him, Stone started the car.

Preston reached across the seat and placed his hand on Stone's thigh, but removed it when he saw his smile slip away. He'd only wanted a connection to the person he'd just kissed, and Stone's reaction confused him. They rode in near silence back to his parents' house, with Preston wondering what he'd done.

Stone pulled the car into the driveway and came to a stop in front of the house. "Thank you for the ride," Preston said, and Stone got out of the car and walked around, helping Preston into his chair before turning around.

Preston reached out and touched his arm gently. He wanted to ask what he'd done wrong. But as he looked into Stone's eyes, what he saw stopped the words in his throat. He let his hand slip away and sat where he was as the car engine started. He didn't go inside until the tail lights disappeared from view.

The front door opened, and he saw his mother standing in the square of light. Without saying anything, he wheeled himself inside and straight to his room. Shrugging off his coat, he threw it on the bed and yanked up the phone, knocking things off the nightstand. "Jasper!"

"Preston? Is your date over already? It's barely nine o'clock."

"Yes. We had a nice dinner and afterwards I kissed him." He could still feel Stone's lips against his, but the memory did nothing to defuse his frustration. "Then he brought me home and left."

"What did you do?" The accusatory tone from his friend only ratcheted things up.

"Nothing. I just kissed him, okay!" God! Why didn't anyone get it? "Stone just dumped me off, and the way he looked at me, Jesus Christ, you'd have thought I was Jack the Ripper or something!" If he could stand, Preston would have been pacing the room, but as it was, all he could do was stew in his chair, and he hated it.

"Slow down." Preston heard Derrick's voice behind Jasper, then he heard Jasper mumble something that obviously wasn't for him. "Give me a minute, and take a deep breath while you're at it." The phone went quiet for a few minutes, and then Jasper returned. "Okay. Now tell me what's got you so upset."

"I already told you."

"Then why don't you start at the beginning?"

"Stone picked me up and we went to the country club for dinner. I wanted to take him someplace nice. We talked about all kinds of stuff. He told me about his family, and I told him about mine." He remembered the way they'd defused the tension and smiled for a second.

"You didn't call him names, did you?"

"Of course not." Preston stopped and thought. "Jasper, I like him," he said softly.

"Ahhh."

"What in hell does that mean?"

"Nothing, go on."

"After dinner, we went to the car and I kissed him, right there in the parking lot, and he kissed me back. It was… special. At least it felt special, and I thought he liked it too." Preston felt his anger start to drain away. "He pulled away, and I put my hand on his thigh. I just wanted to remain in contact with him," he hurried to explain. "But the way he looked at me…." Preston shivered. "That's what being nice gets me, hurt and dumped, again!"

"Christ! You know, Pres, but everything isn't about you! Did you stop to think that he might have reacted that way because of something else other than you? You said you had a good time, right?"

"Yeah, a little heavy, but good. He told me how his dad used to hit him, and then how he threw him out because he was gay."

Love Means ... Freedom

"You've had it easy, Pres. Your mom accepts you, and your dad may not understand, but he didn't throw you out."

"I guess. But Stone looked at me like he was afraid of me."

"Maybe he wasn't afraid of you. Maybe his reaction had nothing to do with you. Did you ever think of that? After his dad threw him out, did he tell you where he was living or what he'd been doing?"

"Not really."

"Pres, being young and alone isn't a picnic, especially when you have nothing. If your parents kicked you out, you'd still have your trust fund and a college education to fall back on." He heard Jasper shift, and a low growly noise came through the phone. "Maybe something happened to him and what you did brought it back, or maybe you just moved too fast for him. I don't have the answer, but he does."

"So what should I do?"

"Try being a friend first and ask him. You like him, right?"

"I do, Jas, I really do. I don't know why, but I do."

"Then put yourself aside and ask him. You were never very patient, but if something did happen to him, he may not be ready to tell you. But follow your heart, it won't lead you astray."

"I'll try."

"Good." Preston was about to hang up. "Oh, and one more thing."

"What?"

"I'm proud of you."

That stopped Preston in his tracks. "What for?" He felt his forehead wrinkle in confusion.

"You'll figure it out."

Preston placed the phone in the cradle, his anger forgotten as he replayed the evening in his mind, looking for clues, but all he kept coming back to was that sweet, unforgettable kiss.

THE lights of the farm appeared on his right. Stone wiped his eyes for what seemed like the millionth time since pulling away from Preston. He knew he'd been operating on adrenaline brought on by near panic, and now that was wearing off, replaced by shame and worry. Pulling into the drive, he parked the car next to one of the trucks and sat still, breathing deeply, trying to regain control of himself. Taking one breath and then another, he looked toward the house, grateful that no one came outside.

After another huge breath and a sigh, he opened the door and climbed out of the car. He took a step and his knees nearly buckled beneath him, but he managed to keep himself upright and walked toward the house.

Entering the back door, the house appeared quiet. He thunked off his shoes and stepped inside, seeing Adelle wiping down the counters, humming quietly to herself.

"You're back so soon?" She must have gotten a good look at him, because Stone found himself guided toward a chair. "Are you okay?"

"No." Stone put his hands over his face to hide his shame.

"Did that boy do something to hurt you? 'Cause I'll whoop him if he did." Stone shook his head. From her tone, he knew she would, too, and it made him feel better in some twisted way.

"He didn't hurt me, not directly, anyway."

Stone heard a chair scrape across the floor. "You lost me." Then he felt hands against his, lightly pulling his fingers away from his face. Rough fingers slid against his palms, holding them tight, massaging lightly.

Stone lifted his gaze and looked into her deep, brown eyes and felt his stomach relax a little. "He kissed me and I liked it."

"There ain't nothin' wrong with that, is there?"

"No, but on the way to his house, he touched my leg." Stone started to shake as everything he'd been trying so desperately to forget

64

Love Means ... Freedom

flooded through him. "I know it sounds stupid, and I think I hurt him and I didn't mean to." He continued shaking, and he felt Adelle's arms around his shoulders, pulling him to her.

"It's okay, Baby Boy, it's okay." Then he was being rocked back and forth like a child, and he clung to her. She didn't ask what had happened, but he told her anyway. The whole story came out in gasps and sobs, and this sweet lady held him through it all. Stone wasn't even sure anyone could understand half the words he'd said, but he'd said them for the first time to another living soul. The entire time, she kept rocking him and holding him, the story sobbing out of him, and when the last terrible details crossed his lips, he held her back and she sang to him, soft and low.

CHAPTER 7

HE COULDN'T move. Strong hands held him down. The man said something. But he couldn't understand, the words seemed blurred through the haze that filled his head. "Stop, please." He was begging. Somehow he managed to turn around and saw the man's face. "Preston, why are you doing this to me?"

Stone gasped, jerking himself awake, covered in sweat, breathing hard like he'd just run the longest race of his life. This had to stop, these dreams had to stop—somehow, someway, he had to make them stop.

STONE shoveled the muck from the stall with muscle-jarring vigor. "If you push any harder, the shovel will go right through the concrete." Stone turned around and saw Geoff standing in the stall doorway, watching him. He didn't say anything more, and Stone didn't feel like talking, so he continued his attack on what the horses left behind. Soon, he no longer felt Geoff's gaze on him, but he didn't really care. The work felt cathartic, and he didn't have to think. For the last few days, since his date with Preston, the dreams had gotten worse, and every time he stopped, his thoughts returned to what he'd done.

Love Means ... Freedom

"Stone!" He stopped and turned around. "Are you there?" He saw Joey smiling teasingly back at him.

"Sorry." He'd been saying that word a lot to everyone lately. He needed to get it together.

"Can you help with Preston's session? I have to go into town and verify the feed order for next year with Geoff."

Stone tried to stifle a groan, but it escaped anyway, and he did his best to cover it up. "Okay." He owed a lot to everyone at the farm and he didn't want to do anything to make them ask him to leave. They'd all treated him like he was family. Not like his family, but how he thought family should treat each other. "Is he riding in the ring?"

"Yes. Belle's already saddled, and all you need to do is continue from the last lesson. His legs are getting stronger, and last time he was able to get on the horse by himself, so he needs to keep working on control." He must have seen the trepidation on Stone's face. "You can do it, I know you can."

"I'll do my best."

"I know you will. The lesson is less than an hour. I have to go, but if you have any problems, call me or Eli on our cells." Joey patted him on the shoulder. "Thank you for doing this for me. I really appreciate it."

Stone nodded as he watched Joey's eyes. There was something wicked in the way his eyes gleamed. Before he could ask what was going on, Joey had already left the barn.

Stone finished cleaning the stall he was working on, inhaling the scent of a fresh barn as he brushed Belle. Her coat flowed beneath his hands as he brushed and groomed her flowing coat of silky hair. "You're a good horse, Belle, just like my Buster." He patted her neck, and she bucked her head like she agreed with him. "Why can't people be like horses?" Of course, he didn't get an answer, but Belle reminded him that even horses were unpredictable when she butted her head against his stomach a little harder than he was expecting. "Thank you, girl." If he didn't know better, he'd have sworn she was smirking at him in her own horsey way.

With Belle groomed, he got her saddle and finished getting her ready for Preston's therapy riding session. Once she was saddled, he walked her to the ring. With each step, his stomach tightened a little more. He knew he had to face Preston and explain what had happened. He also knew that Preston deserved an explanation. Preston would probably hate him once he was done, but after telling Adelle a few days ago, he knew he couldn't hide it inside any more. He deserved to be free of it, regardless of the consequences.

Stone heard the sound of Preston's voice in the barn approaching the ring, and his stomach did another flip-flop. Calming himself, he walked Belle around to Preston so he could slide into the saddle.

Stone watched as Preston stopped talking to Jasper and approached the horse, sliding out of the chair and, to Stone's surprise, standing and managing to take a few steps before Jasper helped guide him onto the horse. He couldn't help smiling at Preston's accomplishment. Once Preston was settled in the saddle, Stone stepped away from Belle. Preston nudged her and she began walking. "Joey said that today he wanted you to work on control, so we'll do some of the same exercises we did last time."

Belle and Preston began moving across the ring, and Stone felt Jasper's hand on his shoulder. Turning to look at him, he saw Jasper motion toward Preston with his head and smile before standing up and walking back through the barn. Stone returned his attention to the horse and rider, steadying his nerves and walking across the ring.

"You're doing very well," Stone commented as he approached, so he wouldn't startle Belle or Preston. "She wants to do what you did last time, so change it up, that way she'll look to you for direction instead of fighting you." Stone watched Preston on Belle. The man looked really good, seated tall and erect, head forward, legs gripping the saddle.

Love Means ... Freedom

Preston rode to the far side of the ring and then turned around and came back toward him. Stone could tell he was being watched, and the feeling got more pronounced as Preston got closer, pulling Belle to a stop. They both looked at each other, not saying anything.

"Can I ask...?"

"Can we talk...?"

They both began at the same time, their questions overlapping. Both of them stopped and smiled before Preston signaled for him to go. "When you're done, could you come back to the house? I think we need to talk."

Preston's expression darkened. "Is this a bad thing?"

Stone didn't know how to answer that question. "Only you can answer that." Stone walked up to the side of the horse, patting her neck as he did. "I do want to say that I'm sorry for how I reacted the other night, and I want you to know it wasn't you." That was true, at least. "This is hard for me to talk about, but I've decided that I'd like to tell you, if you're willing to listen."

"All right." Preston sounded guarded and looked skeptical. Stone figured that was all he could ask for. He'd kept telling himself not to get his hopes up, but as he looked into Preston's eyes, he couldn't help allowing himself a glimmer of hope. He figured he was probably just being stupid, reading way too much into a single act, but that kiss Preston had given him after dinner had stayed with him, and was a big reason he'd decided to confide in him. That and the fact that Adelle had said she'd whoop him if need be.

Stone stepped back from the horse. "I saw that you were able to stand?"

"Uh-huh, I can stand for small periods."

"Then let's see if you can handle a trot. It's a little faster and requires a lot more balance and coordination with the horse. It'll also use your legs more than walking, so we'll only do it for a short period of time." Preston got Belle moving and then nudged her again, and she

69

began a light trot around the ring. "Don't bounce on her, move with her and use your legs." It took a few minutes, but Preston began to get the hang of it. Horse and rider began to move together. "How are your legs?"

"Getting tired."

Stone wasn't surprised. Preston was beginning to look like he'd had a workout. "Then slow her to a walk." Preston pulled back on the reins. "That's it. You did great. Walk her over here and we'll get you back in your chair." Preston walked Belle over and pulled his leg over, sliding with Stone's help into his chair. "You've come a long way in a short time."

"When I'm up there, riding, I feel normal, like I'm just like everyone else. I hate this fucking chair." He slapped the arm. "I want to be normal again."

Stone knelt next to the chair. "You will be. Your legs are already stronger. Trotting is hard work, and you did it today. You couldn't have done that if your legs weren't getting stronger. It just takes time and patience." Something Stone didn't think Preston had in abundance.

Preston turned, looking at Stone, their lips so close together. Stone felt him lean toward him, but he backed away. "Please." The nerves were back with a vengeance. "Let me say what I have to say. Then you can decide if I'm someone you want to be kissing."

Further conversation was cut off by the sound of a pair of running feet and the squeal of a young voice. "Stoney!" He looked up and saw Sherry racing toward him. Before he could stand, she nearly bowled him over and she threw herself into his arms. "Mama says I get to ride today."

"Yes, you do."

She looked into the ring. "Do I get to ride her?" Sherry's eyes got huge—Belle was bigger than Mercury, the pony she was used to riding.

"You'll have to ask Mr. Eli when he comes."

She stood right next to him, holding on to him and looking expectantly at the door to the barn and then at her mother. Stone could feel that she wasn't exactly completely comfortable, but as long as mom was nearby, she seemed to be fine. She pointed and whispered, "What's her name?" Stone whispered it back to her, and she laughed as her mother approached. "Mama, guess what. That horse's name is Tinkerbelle." Eli joined the group walking in from the barn leading Mercury.

"I think maybe you should keep riding Mercury for a while, he'll miss you." That seemed to make her ponder a minute, and then she let her mother lead her toward the pony.

Stone felt a slap on his leg. "You've had me riding Tinkerbelle!" Preston's eyes were smiling, belying the mock anger in his voice.

"Yup, I was wondering when you'd figure it out." Stone looked into the ring, and Eli motioned that he could go. So after waving to Sherry, he followed Preston through the barn, grabbing his coat before walking outside and to the back door.

The house was completely quiet. Everyone was out, and even Adelle was conspicuously absent. Without thinking, he led them into the living room and flopped onto the sofa. "Would you help me out of this thing?" They got Preston settled on one end of the sofa, and Stone settled himself on the other. His stomach was doing flips as he wondered where to start, then he figured he might as well get this over with so that Preston would leave and he could figure out what to do next.

"About six months ago, I met Jacob. He was new in school, and I fell for him hard."

"What happened?" Preston's voice was so soft.

"The usual, I guess. He graduated with me and went away to college. I found out he was just playing around, and that I was convenient, I guess." Stone sighed, figuring this had happened to lots of guys. "I was really stupid and decided I needed to be honest, so I told my dad I was gay."

71

"I know exactly how you felt, and you weren't stupid, just honest and tired of hiding." Preston's eyes showed that the sentiment was genuine, and Stone relaxed enough to continue.

Stone's jaw tightened, and he mentally fortified himself. "I didn't know he'd been drinking, but I shouldn't have been surprised. He got it in his mind that he could beat my gayness out of me. He whipped off his belt and began beating me with it. Thankfully, as drunk as he was, he ran out of steam and just started yelling and screaming that if I was still here, he'd give me more of the same." Stone knew his voice was soft, but he couldn't talk any louder or he felt like he'd be broadcasting his shame.

He heard Preston mutter under his breath something that sounded like, "The bastard."

"I took what I could and left while he was still passed out. I wasn't sure where to go, so I called Uncle Pete. He's a man I've known all my life and someone I thought was a friend."

"Oh no." Preston muttered softly, his hand going to his mouth, and Stone nodded slowly.

"Your dad will calm down once he sobers up." Peter stood in his kitchen, yawning. "I'll get some blankets for the couch."

"Thanks for letting me stay." Stone felt miserable, and his back ached terribly. He hadn't known where to go, and Uncle Pete was like a second father to him.

"No problem, kid." The use of his old nickname was reassuring. "Turn off the lights when you go to bed." Pete walked away, and Stone thought he'd found a safe place, at least for a while. Arranging the blankets, he climbed into the warm cocoon and prayed his "uncle" was right and that his dad would understand. After staring at the ceiling, he eventually dropped off.

Stone woke abruptly to a weight on his legs. Then the blankets slid off and he shivered in the cold room. "Come on, Stone, be good to your Uncle Pete." Instantly awake, he was too startled to fight at first,

Love Means ... Freedom

but when he felt hands slide up his thighs and his underwear slide down his legs, he began to struggle.

"Come on, Stone." His voice was almost seductive. "You're gonna like this." Weight pressed him against the sofa, flipping him onto his stomach, face smashed against the cushion, held by one hand while the other pawed at him. He gasped and tried to scream as he struggled against the bigger man's superior weight. "This is what you want! I'm only giving you what you want," his uncle began repeating, before lips wet his ear and the paw slid beneath his cheeks.

"Don't do this, please," Stone begged, but he wasn't sure if he'd actually tried to vocalize the words or if he'd just uttered them in his mind. But the effect was the same, a plea ignored as something hard slid along his skin, and he bucked back again and again trying somehow to get the other man off him, but he was too big and heavy.

Then he felt something try to push into him. The pain was unlike anything he'd ever felt, and his head filled with screams. The pressure backed away, and Stone braced for the worst and felt a hot wetness on his skin, with his uncle breathing heavily in his ear.

The weight slipped off him, and all Stone wanted to do was disappear off the face of the earth. He wanted to die. "I was only giving you what you wanted." He heard footsteps on the floor, then laughter, as if he was reading Stone's thoughts. "Not as though anyone will believe you anyway." Then a door closed, and Stone lay breathing heavily as the wetness ran down his legs.

Stone lay on the sofa, making sure the house was quiet. He grabbed one of the blankets and did his best to clean himself up. Sliding his clothes on, he continued listening, but the house was still.

"I sat awake for the rest of the night, but only after I found something to use as a weapon, and as soon as it started getting light, I grabbed my stuff and ran out of the house, taking the money I knew he hid in a jar in the kitchen." Stone felt wrung out, but he couldn't stop now. He had to finish this.

"What did you do? Where did you go?" Preston swallowed hard, and Stone looked at his face, expecting to see pity, but couldn't read anything at all.

"I walked the entire day and happened upon a farm south of town that was looking for people to help cut Christmas trees." Stone's glance moved to the decorated tree in the corner of the room, and he couldn't stop the shiver. He'd never look at a Christmas tree the same way again. "When the trees were cut, they found work for me as long as they could." Stone inhaled and sighed. "I started moving south, hitching rides where I could, walking a lot. I didn't care where I went as long as it was towards south and hopefully warmer."

Stone could feel Preston's gaze on his, eyes locked onto his, expression betraying nothing, and Stone felt his nerves fall away and the tears that had threatened dry up. He'd cried enough already and he wasn't going to do it again—not in front of Preston if he could help it. "I got a few rides, but many of the guys who picked me up demanded payment." Stone swallowed and found he couldn't hold Preston's gaze any more.

"What kind of payment…?" Preston's eyes got wide.

"Yeah, that kind of payment." Stone stared at his legs. "I felt like such worthless shit, I did it a few times just to stay warm and keep moving. The last time, I just couldn't do it, and the driver threw me out just down the road. I nearly froze to death trying to find shelter, and then I saw the lights from the farm." Stone got up and began walking away, standing in the doorway to the kitchen. "See why I knew you wouldn't want to be kissing me? I'm a guy who sucked cock to get rides. Damaged goods." Stone looked anywhere but at Preston. "I'm sure someone can get you home." It was better for things to end now before he got really hurt. Stone began walking away.

"Do you see me as damaged?" Preston asked softly, and Stone stopped in his tracks.

"No." He didn't turn around.

"I used to. I still do in some ways." Preston's voice remained level and soft.

"You're not damaged. You'll walk again and be as good as new. As perfect and handsome as you ever were." Stone's voice cracked, and he covered it with a cough. "I'll always be a whore who sold himself for a ride." He crushed his eyes shut, trying to hold back the emotions.

"Stone." Preston called softly, and he turned around, seeing that Preston held out his hand. "I'd come to you if I could." Stone slowly walked closer. "You're not damaged any more than I am. Your 'uncle' did more than attack you—he tried to steal your peace of mind. You can let him win or you can move on with your life." Stone let Preston's voice guide him back onto the sofa.

"That doesn't change the fact that I whored myself." Stone watched Preston's chest rise and fall, waiting. Then the man actually rolled his eyes, and Stone went off. "You arrogant bastard!"

To Stone's surprise, Preston laughed. "That's what they keep telling me."

Stone couldn't hold onto his anger. "Well, they're right."

"Maybe, but it has its place. You stopped feeling sorry for yourself, at least for a second." Stone wanted to snack that smug look off the man's face, either that or kiss it away.

"As long as you promise to use it for good." Stone returned Preston's smirk.

"And how do you suggest I do that?" Preston raised his eyebrow in a gesture he probably thought was suggestive, but came off more like Groucho Marx.

"I'll let you know." Stone felt Preston's hand against his cheek.

"You do that." The low tone sent a shiver of desire through him. He didn't have time to think how quickly Preston had made him forget everything else but him and his hands, the warmth reaching his body through their clothes.

Slowly, Preston leaned toward Stone, giving him time to pull away if he wanted. Stone felt his heart start to pound again and nearly backed away as their lips touched lightly. "You're not damaged, Stone." Fuck, that voice was seductive. The kiss deepened, and he went with it, loving the tingly feeling that shot through his body. Stone felt that Preston was holding back, and for that, he was very grateful. They just kissed softly, tenderly, lips saying hello and hearts reaching out to each other in those first tentative steps. Then Stone felt the kiss gentle further and fade away.

Stone smiled, and it was his turn to lean in, returning Preston's gesture with one of his own. An arm hugged him lightly, and they kissed again, slowly, almost timidly. Stone was unsure, and Preston must have thought the younger man would bolt if he went too fast, so they both took their time before parting again. "On the twenty-fourth, Geoff has a get-together planned for friends, and he said I could bring someone if I want." Stone chewed his lower lip, wondering. "Would you like to come?"

"What time should I be here?" Preston smiled and captured Stone's lips again. This time, the kiss was more forceful, deeper, and Stone felt the passion start to build. He was still leery of starting anything too physical, but Preston seemed content with kissing. Something in his mind wondered how long Preston would be willing to wait. He wasn't the most patient person... but Stone pushed those concerns aside for now. He'd taken the first step and it felt good. He couldn't help thinking that there were others around the corner that wouldn't be so easy.

Their kiss ended, and Stone surprised himself when he didn't jerk away as Preston pulled him close, hands on his stomach, allowing him to rest against his chest. It had been such a long time since he'd been held this way, and it felt nice.

CHAPTER 8

"WHO in the fuck"—Preston moved one foot forward, huffing—
"schedules a therapy"—now the other foot came forward—"session
on"—yet another step and a gasp through clenched teeth—"fucking
Christmas Eve?" He reached the end of the bars and turned himself
around.

"I believe that was you." Jasper actually had the gall to smile, and
Preston took a swipe at him before beginning the long, sixteen-foot trek
to the other end.

"Well, fuck you, anyway." Preston made his way to the other end,
gasping for breath and groaning the entire time. "How do babies ever
learn to do this shit, anyway?" He turned around again.

"This time, stop in the middle," Jasper instructed, and Preston
walked another eight feet, hands steadying on the bars. "Good. That's
the best you've ever done. Now I want you to stand on both feet and let
go of the bars. I'm going to time you to see how long you can stand,
but as soon as you touch the bars, it's over."

"Okay, sadist," Preston mock-grumbled as he placed his feet and
released his hands. He felt unsteady and wobbled initially, but
compensated.

"See, you're standing on your own. Thirty seconds." Jasper marked the time. "I understand you're spending the evening with Stone."

"Yeah." He smiled, looking forward to seeing him again and maybe kissing under the mistletoe. "Mom was disappointed that I wouldn't be home tonight, but she understood. She and Dad are visiting relatives anyway." He felt one leg start to vibrate, but held it steady, trying to remain standing.

"Did you get him anything?" Jasper looked at the clock and smiled. "Two minutes. You're doing great."

"I think so. I wasn't really sure what to get him, and I wanted something nice." Preston's leg began to buckle and he grabbed the bar, steadying himself before slowly making his way back to the chair. Once he was seated, he rolled himself over to his coat, dug in his pocket for a box, and handed it to Jasper. "I noticed he doesn't have one."

Jasper peeked inside and handed it back. "Very nice. I think you did great both with the gift and standing. You got over three minutes, and at the end of the session. You're doing really well."

"Thanks." He smiled and put the box back in his pocket. "I'll be walking in no time."

"You certainly will." Jasper picked up his coat and flipped the therapy studio light switch. "Let's get you home so you can clean up. I'll take you to the farm, and then I have a present I need to give Derrick." The look on his face was lecherous.

"From what I hear, you'll be the one doing the getting," Preston teased, and Jasper smiled, leading the way out of the building and across the now empty parking lot to his car.

Preston got himself settled and they rode home. Preston led the way into the house, wheeling himself toward his room. The house was quiet, his parents apparently already gone. "I'll shower and then we can go."

Love Means ... Freedom

"No problem, just don't take forever." Jasper snickered. Preston knew as well as he that it took him awhile no matter how fast he tried to move.

"Ha, ha." He handed Jasper the box for Stone. "Would you wrap that for me while I'm cleaning up? The stuff's in the office."

"Sure." Jasper moved toward the indicated room. "Get going already."

Preston moved toward his room, pulling off his coat and shedding his clothes as quickly as he could before wheeling himself naked into the bathroom. His shower had been specially equipped, and he absolutely hated the thing. He used it because he had to, but all the special accommodations made him angry—he just wanted to be normal, whole again. Preston moved to the bathing seat and started the water. The water felt good as it washed over him, and Preston let himself wonder what it would be like to have Stone in here with him. "I'd bet you'd be stunning," he said to himself as he brought up a picture of the young man in his mind. Skin all wet, hair slicked down. In his mind, he pictured him with smooth skin and long, wiry legs. Maybe they could put this freaking seat to more interesting uses?

Preston found that part of him had no trouble whatsoever standing, and he had to stop himself from jacking off thinking about Stone. He didn't have time, and if he hurried, he'd have more time to spend with the handsome creature he was imagining. "No fair beating off in there," Jasper called from his bedroom.

"Very funny. I'll be done in a second. Keep your pants on, because I sure don't want to see you naked." He heard laughter and the door closed again. Preston's arousal had abated enough that he could finish cleaning himself, turning off the water before drying as best he could and transferring back to his chair. Preston managed to get his underwear and pants on before finally deciding on a festive red shirt. Pulling on socks and shoes, he grabbed the coat he wanted to wear and wheeled back to the living room. "Do I look okay?"

Jasper stood and grabbed his coat before looking Preston over appraisingly. "You look very nice." He handed Preston the beautifully wrapped package, and they left the house.

Traffic was heavy as they drove through town, but thinned expectedly as they made their way down country roads toward the farm. "You don't need me to pick you up, do you?"

Preston smiled. "No. Stone said he'd bring me home." They pulled into the drive and pulled to a stop. "Thank you, Jas, Merry Christmas." They'd already exchanged gifts, so he hugged him tight.

"Merry Christmas, Pres." Jasper held him and didn't immediately let go. "You know the chair doesn't define who you are." Preston pulled back, wondering where Jasper was going. "Remember the person you were before the accident."

"You mean the one who could walk, take himself to the bathroom, and get people to look at me once in a while with something other than pity?" Preston remarked sarcastically.

"No, you big ass! I mean the guy who could enliven a party just by coming in the door, the guy who had fun, and the guy who drove Old Man Newkirk to an early retirement." They both smiled at the memory. "That guy is still in there somewhere. And if you see pity when people look at you, it's because of the attitude, not the chair." Jasper pointed toward the house. "So get in there and show them the Preston I know and love."

He folded his hands over his chest, not sure if he was insulted or if Jasper was being purposely condescending. "Which one is that?"

Jasper grinned and then began to laugh. "The adult version of the guy who, sophomore year, convinced every freshman on the football team that on November first, it was a school tradition to wear their jockstraps on the outside of their uniforms." Jasper began laughing hysterically, and Preston couldn't stop himself and laughed right along with him, a deep belly laugh that he hadn't experienced in months.

Love Means ... Freedom

"They nearly killed me," Preston gasped. He hadn't thought of that in years.

"But the pictures were great blackmail." Their laughter drifted away, but the smiles remained.

"Thanks." He looked over at what he suddenly realized was the best friend he'd ever had. "Let me go so you can get home to that man of yours."

Preston was still smiling as he got himself in his chair, and Stone rushed out and helped him into the house, both of them waving as Jasper drove away. It had started to snow on the drive over, the landscape being covered in a fresh blanket of white, like nature wanted everything fresh and clean for the holiday. "Let's get you inside."

"Not yet, okay?" Preston wasn't cold, and they sat quietly, watching the snow fall. Looking over at Stone, Preston took the younger man's hand in his and held it, fingers sharing their warmth. It had been a long time since he'd simply held hands with anyone. Kent was a more... active kind of guy. Basically, Kent had been all about the sex, jackrabbit-type sex, always a race to the finish. But sitting with Stone watching it snow was one of the nicest things he could remember. "Are the horses inside?"

Stone met his eyes before his gaze drifted to the barn. "Yup, all snug and warm inside, which is where we should be as well." Preston nodded, and Stone helped him up the steps and into the kitchen.

Warmth assailed him as he took off his coat and glided into the kitchen. Eli was still getting everything ready, and fresh bread was being pulled from the oven.

"Man, that smells good."

Eli smiled as he closed the over door and put the bread on a rack to cool. "I used to work in my uncle's bakery." Eli continued working.

"Is there anything I can do to help?"

Eli looked like he was about to say no. "There is, actually. Do you think you could make the punch?" Getting out the fixings from the refrigerator, Eli placed them on the counter and told him how to mix it. "Stone, would you bring up a few chairs and set them in the living room?" Eli asked, and Stone hurried away. It seemed there was still a lot to do.

Preston carried the ingredients to the punch bowl and began mixing them together. Geoff came in to ask a question and was given his answer and another thing to do. It seemed for this, Eli was in charge. By the time Preston was finished, Adelle joined them and began hauling more food to the table. It looked like they were expecting an army, and it wasn't long before one arrived. Geoff's aunts, cousins, their children, some of the men he'd seen around the farm. He was introduced to one and all, including a woman and her young daughter.

"We can't stay long," the woman explained, "but Sherry insisted we stop by so she could give Mr. Stoney his present." The woman's smile lit the room.

Preston watched as Stone knelt down, and the little girl gave him a big hug before handing him a drawing she'd obviously made herself. "Thank you, Sherry." Stone returned the little girl's hug. "Is that Mercury?"

"Uh-huh," she said in her little voice, nodding vigorously. "And that's you on Buster." She seemed so proud of it, and he could tell Stone was a little choked up as he looked away from the little girl, trying to hide the stab of pain and loneliness that crossed his face.

"Sherry, this is Preston." Stone said, and the little girl looked at him wide-eyed.

"Can you go fast?" she asked, pointing at his big wheels.

"Sometimes. Would you like a ride?"

Sherry looked up at her mother, who nodded, and then she climbed onto Preston's lap and Stone pushed them around the house

Love Means ... Freedom

while Sherry laughed and urged them to go faster, dodging legs and howling with glee. After a few times around the house, they returned to the kitchen to find every kid lined up for his or her turn. Sherry turned and hugged him before sliding off his lap and walking to her mother, who wiped her eyes and looked at Stone.

"I can't believe what you've done for her." She lifted Sherry into her arms. "What you've all done for her." She looked primarily at Stone and said, "Thank you." She sniffed, and Sherry settled in her arms. "We should go." She set Sherry down, and she put on her pink puffy coat and then said good-bye again, giving "Stoney" a hug before leaving, waving her tiny hand the entire time.

"Can I have a ride?" one of the young boys asked before climbing on Preston's lap for a spin around the house. It was wonderful being the source of fun again, even if it was because of the damned chair.

After all the youngsters had had a turn, Preston glided into the living room, settling to a stop next to the sofa, listening to bits of conversation. He knew all too well that the chair made a lot of people uncomfortable, and he wasn't surprised that the conversation swirled around him but didn't tend to include him.

"Are you having a good time?" Preston turned and saw Robbie sitting on the sofa next to him. A hand with long slender fingers felt for his arm. "I always have trouble at parties. Too many voices and moving objects," he stage whispered, to Preston's amusement. Joey sat next to his partner and handed him a plate, and Preston listened as Joey explained where everything was.

Preston sighed and craned his neck, looking around the room. He couldn't see Stone, but he saw Geoff and Eli standing together, with Geoff's arm around Eli's waist, talking to Len and Chris, the two of them holding hands, and of course, Joey and Robbie sitting on the sofa, like Siamese twins joined at the hip. "You okay?" Stone's voice startled him.

"Sure." What was he going to say? That he was feeling lonely, wishing he had someone the way everyone else seemed to? Like that was going to happen as long as he was in the chair. Sure, Stone had gone out with him and invited him to the party, but he still couldn't see anyone wanting to be with a cripple.

Stone pulled up a chair, setting it next to his. "Would you like something to eat? I'll get you a plate if you like."

"No, thank you." He wasn't particularly hungry.

"Are you sure? I know it's hard with all the people around." Stone's concern seemed so genuine and caring, his eyes so big and earnest, that Preston relented and smiled as Stone bounded off his chair and made off toward the food.

Preston watched Stone move, those pants he was wearing hugging that tight little butt.

"Enjoying yourself?" He'd been so engrossed watching Stone, he hadn't noticed Geoff approach.

"Very much. Thank you for having me." He smiled and Geoff smiled back, but neither of them seemed to know what to say. Geoff stood, shifting his weight from leg to leg, and Preston looked around the room trying to figure out a way to ask what he wanted to ask. "Stone had to leave his horse behind."

"I know he's been worried about him."

"I was wondering—after the holiday, could you help me get Buster for him? I can't really drive, and he needs his horse. I know he worries about him a lot."

Geoff looked at him like he had three heads. And then his expression softened as he followed Preston's gaze back to Stone. "I see."

"Huh?"

"Nothing, sorry." Geoff fumbled for a second. "Actually, that's a good idea. Let me check to see who actually owns Buster. If he's not

Love Means ... Freedom

legally Stone's, then there might be a problem. But, yeah, I think that's just what Stone needs."

"What is it I need?" Stone sounded defensive, handing Preston his plate before folding his hands over his chest. Preston reached out to him, but Geoff put an arm around his shoulder first.

"Preston was just asking me if after the holidays we could get Buster for you," Geoff replied, and Stone's face lit in a huge smile, his arms slipping to his sides.

"For real?" He could barely contain his excitement.

"Uh-huh. But we need to know who really owns Buster."

Almost before Geoff had finished his thought, Stone was gone, his footsteps tromping up the stairs, and a few minutes later he raced back down the stairs, carrying a yellow piece of paper. "I had it with my papers and grabbed it with my stuff." He handed it to Geoff. "It's the bill of sale for Buster."

Geoff looked at the document and grinned. "Perfect, it's in your name, so he can't legally stop you. As soon as we have good weather, we'll head north to get your horse."

Stone alternated his gaze between both men, looking like he'd just gotten the greatest Christmas present ever. As Geoff drifted off to visit with his other guests, Stone sat in the chair next to Preston, and they ate and talked until the tree began to sparkle brighter and the light through the windows began to fade.

"Good night," Len and Chris said to both of them, each shaking his hand and giving Stone a hug. "Merry Christmas." Their exit began the exodus, and everyone said their good-nights, exchanging hugs and promising to get together later.

"I should take you home," Stone said as the house quieted to the sounds of cleanup, and Preston heard Adelle shooing everyone out of her kitchen.

Preston bundled himself up to go outside, wishing everyone a Merry Christmas before managing to make it to the car. Snow was now coming down hard and the wind was blowing, swirling the snow around the car. Stone started the car, turning on the radio, and Christmas music filled the car: *"Let it snow, let it snow, let it snow."*

"Drive carefully and call before you start back."

Stone said he would and rolled up the window, pulling away and out onto the street, flashes of white coming at them through the headlights like tiny, white bullets. Preston didn't talk, watching the road and letting Stone concentrate. Turning the corner, heading south, the snow began blowing across them. "Shit, shit!!"

Preston snapped his head around to Stone, wondering what was wrong.

"I forgot to give you your present."

Preston's hand went to his own coat pocket and the wrapped box that was still there. He'd give it to Stone when they reached the house. "You got me a present?" Preston found himself inordinately pleased that Stone had thought of him.

The car swerved, and Stone's attention focused back on the road. "Damn, I can't see a thing," he murmured as he got the car back under control.

"I know, and it seems to be getting worse." The gifts were forgotten as they both concentrated on the road and the flakes filling the headlight beams.

The music ended on the radio. "The National Weather Service has issued a blizzard warning for Mason, Osceola, and Manistee counties. Heavy lake effect snow combined with high winds has reduced visibility and is causing extreme whiteout conditions. Officials warn that road conditions are deteriorating fast and that only emergency travel should be attempted." The announcement ended and *The First Noel* began to play.

Love Means ... Freedom

"This came up fast." Stone glanced at Preston and then back at the road. "And I thought storms came up fast in Petoskey." He slowed the car to a crawl. "What should we do?"

"Turn around and go back to the farm." They'd only gone a few miles, and even if they made it to the house, Stone would never make it back. His parents were probably stuck as well, and while being alone in the house with Stone was a very pleasant thought, he didn't want to take any chances. "We've only gone a few miles."

"But it's Christmas. Your family...."

Preston's first and only thought was of Stone. "We need to go back. The roads are getting worse, and you won't make it back. Remember, it's going to be worse the closer we get to the lake." The car stopped, and Stone turned right in the street. "Be careful of the shoulder on this side." The wind had already drifted across parts of both lanes, narrowing the roadway considerably, and it took awhile to get the car turned around and moving forward again in the sea of white.

"I feel bad that you'll miss Christmas."

Preston wasn't particularly worried. "I'm not missing Christmas. I'll just be spending it with you." He looked across the seat. "I mean... if that's okay." They continued moving through the whipping snow, barely able to see the street at all. "Is it foggy too?"

"No, that's more blowing snow." Stone's phone rang, and he handed it to Preston and continued their slow crawl back to the farm.

"Stone." He heard Geoff's voice. "Where are you?"

"It's Preston. We're on our way back. I think we're coming up on the turn to the farm."

"We'll look for you. I've got all the lights on." Geoff hung up, and it seemed like forever until they made the corner and then the short distance to the drive. Turning in, Stone pulled as close as he could and turned off the engine, breathing an audible sigh of relief. The back door opened, and Geoff, Eli, and Adelle came rushing out. The car had

87

barely stopped when doors were opened. Eli took out Preston's chair and headed for the house. Before he could complain—and he wanted to—Geoff had his door open and an arm under his legs and behind his back, lifting him out of the car.

"I…." Preston started to protest, but the wind blew right through his coat and clothes to his skin. It was much stronger than it had been when they'd left not half an hour earlier. Geoff got him inside and into a chair at the table, and his phone began to ring.

"Preston, where are you? Are you okay?" His mother sounded frantic.

"I'm at the farm. We tried to make it home, but turned around," he explained, watching Adelle shrug off her coat and start working at the stove.

He could hear his mother sigh with relief. "We still at your aunt's. It's bad here too."

Preston felt his own tension slip away. He hated that she'd worried. "I'm glad you're safe. I'll call you tomorrow. Merry Christmas, Mom, and wish everyone there a Merry Christmas for me." To his surprise, he heard her sniffle. "What's wrong? We're all safe and we'll be together soon."

"I know, but you're still my baby and I worry." She did sound better now. "I kept calling and you didn't answer." He glanced at the display: six missed calls.

"I'm sorry. I left it in my coat and didn't hear it." He talked to her for a few more minutes until his dad came on, and they talked a little before wishing each other a Merry Christmas and hanging up.

"Are they okay?" Stone set a cup in front of him.

Preston explained where they were. He felt Stone's hand on his shoulder, helping him get his coat off, and he leaned back against his touch, surprised at how much he craved it. Once his coat was off, Preston reached into his pocket and pulled out the gift, asking Stone to

Love Means ... Freedom

place it under the tree, and he smiled at the delighted look on Stone's face.

It wasn't long before Joey, Geoff, and Eli came back in from checking on the animals. Preston saw Robbie join them as well, and everyone sat around the table as Adelle dished up plates of Heaven and joined them. "Merry Christmas, everyone. You're all welcome, and we're all pleased to be together." Glasses clinked, and Preston felt something he hadn't felt since leaving school—truly included.

Preston glanced around as happy, excited conversation swirled around the table, and it hit him in the stomach, in the best way possible. These people, whom he'd only known a few weeks, accepted him. Robbie was blind, and except for gentle guidance, he was treated the same as everyone else. He'd seen it at the party, and he saw it again just now as Joey guided his hand to the glass and explained how his food was situated on his plate. And Robbie had a job at the farm. When he'd found out that the person in charge of the therapy program was blind, he'd been blown away, and now he understood where it came from— the support of these people. And that was what he wanted. As Preston watched, Robbie laughed as Joey said something in his ear, and Robbie bumped Joey's shoulder back playfully. His gaze drifted to Stone, smile full, eyes bright, laughing with his... family. That was what he wanted, and he realized he hoped he could have, with Stone.

Once everyone was stuffed to the gills with Adelle's southern cooking and the dishes were in the sink, they drifted into the living room. Preston looked expectantly at the large television, but was surprised when Joey handed Robbie his violin and he began to play. *Oh Holy Night, Silent Night, It Came Upon a Midnight Clear,* all flowed from its strings.

Stone began to sing, quietly at first, a clear tenor voice, his ringing tone mixing with Robbie's strings. Preston turned and moved closer, drawn to the sound Stone was making, watching those full lips in rapt fascination as they formed the sounds for the lyrics. The final chord held and died away. Stone's voice was now silent, and Preston leaned against him, placing the gentle touch of his lips on Stone's cheek.

The spell lasted until Robbie broke into a rousing rendition of *Jingle Bells*, with everyone singing raucously and swaying together in one expression of joy that seemed to fill the room and burst into the snowy night beyond.

This was the most Christmas fun he'd had in years, and he tried not to think of the subdued celebrations he had at home. This was loud, raucous at times, and so much fun: singing, cookies, games, and still more food, all happening around the sparkle of the tree decked with rustic ornaments, orchestrated by Robbie's violin. Quite frankly, he didn't want it to end, but he stifled a yawn that caused another.

"We should head to bed," Geoff said to Eli, who nodded and yawned widely. "Chores have to be done in the morning."

Joey and Robbie said their goodnights and headed upstairs together. Preston watched the dog that had been sleeping in one of the corners get up and follow them upstairs, with two cats trailing behind.

"If you'll bring me some blankets, I can sleep here." Preston didn't want to put anyone out, and he couldn't navigate the stairs.

"Geoff, could you take him upstairs? He can have my bed and I'll sleep here," Stone offered softly. "He'll be more comfortable there." Stone gave him a look that said this was going to be a fight if he disagreed, so Preston found himself back in Geoff's arms. The surprisingly strong man carried him upstairs, with Stone following, carrying up his chair. At the top of the stairs, Stone unfolded his chair, and Geoff set Preston in it, saying good night and then disappearing back down the stairs.

"Do you need any help?" Stone showed him the bathroom. His first reflex was to say no, but he wasn't sure if he'd need anything. The bathroom wouldn't have any of the hated modifications that he'd come to rely on.

"I'm not sure."

"Then I'll stay here in the hall. Call if you need me." Stone must have seen the embarrassment that welled through Preston, because he smoothed his hand over his arm. "My mom used to tell me that we all need help every once in a while."

Preston nodded, wheeled himself into the bathroom, and cleaned up with no issues. When he was done, he glided out backwards and met Stone, who directed him to the bedroom.

"You should have everything you need. There are clean sheets on the bed." He turned back the covers. "I'll see you in the morning." The door began to close behind him.

"Stone." The door opened, and he poked his head back inside. "Please." Preston held out his hand, looking to Stone, waiting to see if he'd accept the invitation. Preston wanted desperately to know what Stone felt like. "Don't sleep on the sofa."

Stone moved slowly into the room, and Preston breathed a sigh that he hadn't been rejected. He'd half expected it, anyway. Their hands touched, and Preston gently tugged Stone to him, his other hand tracing the skin on his cheek, thumb sliding over a quivering lower lip. "Don't be scared or nervous. I'd never hurt you, ever." The force of the sentiment behind the words was almost scary in its vehemence. "I promise."

Stone nodded, and Preston let his hands slip away and opened his shirt, letting it slip off his shoulders before sliding off his shoes and getting his socks off his feet. Reclining on the bed, he slid off his pants, leaving his underwear on and shimmying beneath the crisp, cool covers. Stone hadn't taken his eyes off Preston.

The covers lifted and cool air reached Preston's skin, replaced by Stone's furnacelike warmth. "It's been...." Stone's voice a little shaky.

"I know. Don't worry, just relax." He put his arm over Stone's tummy and drew them together, Stone resting in the crook of his body.

It felt so good to hold someone again, to hear Stone's soft breathing and feel his warmth.

Preston let his hand wander, making small circles on Stone's smooth stomach, his reward a soft moan.

"I don't want you to go when we get Buster."

Preston's hand stopped moving, and he began to move away as Stone rolled over. The hurt welled inside him and he almost lashed out, but stopped himself.

"My dad can be a mean bastard and he might hurt you," Stone's eyes drifted to the pillow. "Particularly if he thinks you mean something to me."

"Do I? Mean something to you?" Preston held his breath and lightly ran his hand beneath Stone's chin, needing to see those eyes, even in the dim light.

"Yes."

Preston relaxed and began stroking along Stone's hip. "I can take care of myself, and I really want to go." He felt his own eyes narrow. "If he gives you grief, he'll have to deal with me." He let his voice soften and said, "Because you mean something to me too." What, he wasn't completely sure. He wouldn't let himself call it love, not yet. Stone was so young, so inexperienced, and if he didn't shelter his heart, he was afraid he'd get it broken again. Kent hadn't been right for him, he knew that now, but that only convinced him that his choices in men were suspect. Trying not to let those thoughts intrude on the bubble of warmth that surrounded them, he kissed Stone lightly at first, but easily found himself drawn deeper by the intoxicating taste of the man pressed so close to him.

"Okay." Stone returned his kiss before rolling over, and Preston again held him close, face near his shoulder, warmth surrounding them. "Merry Christmas, Preston." A hand slid along Preston's leg, his nerves firing, excitement growing. To his relief, Stone didn't pull away as his erection rested against warm cheeks.

Love Means ... freedom

Taking a chance, he slid his hand down and found that Stone was equally excited. He wanted to know what Stone sounded like when he was excited, passion filling him, wanted to know what he looked like when he came, tasted like when he couldn't hold back. But this wasn't the time. Stone had to know that he could trust Preston, and he figured the best way to do that was to take time and be patient, something he'd never done before—and maybe that was the problem. "Merry Christmas, Stone." And it was, the merriest one he could remember. He moved his hand away, but kept it firmly around the man he was coming to care for.

CHAPTER 9

"ARE you ready to go?" Geoff asked, leaning against the front of the truck as Stone came down the steps.

"As I'll ever be." He really wasn't sure about this. He wanted to get Buster, there was no doubt about that, he just wished it didn't involve seeing his father. Approaching the truck, he pulled open the door and climbed inside. "You don't have to do this."

The driver's door slammed closed, and Geoff looked over at him, his expression steely. "I know I don't. This farm is a family, and like it or not," Geoff said, now smiling, "you're a member of it, and we help and support one another."

Holy fuck. These people he'd met a few weeks ago considered him family and treated him better than his own had ever done. "I don't know what to say."

"You don't have to say anything. Now let's pick up Preston so we can get going." Geoff started the engine and pulled the truck, with the horse trailer behind, out onto the road. "Have you got the bill of sale?" Stone patted his backpack on the floor between his legs. "Good. And I know that Adelle packed us enough food to last for three days."

"That she did." He patted his full stomach. "I think she's trying to fatten me up."

"When she first got here, I swear I put on ten pounds in a month. Eli's a good baker, but she can cook, and her fried chicken and cornbread are sent from Heaven." He mimicked Robbie's southern accent as he stole his phrase.

The truck bounded down the country road and approached the main highway, and Geoff turned toward Ludington. It didn't take long and then they were pulling into Preston's driveway. As they pulled up, the front door opened and Preston glided outside, followed by his mother. Geoff stopped the truck and turned off the engine, both of them getting out. "Do you boys have everything you need? I can make you sandwiches," she offered, her smile genuine.

"No, thank you, we're good," Geoff replied, and he shook her hand, introducing himself while Stone got Preston out of his chair and into the truck.

"Mom, I'll call you later and let you know what's going on," Preston called from the cab as Stone got in and Geoff walked around the truck. As Geoff started the truck, Preston waved and they pulled out of the driveway.

"Your mother seems like a nice lady," Geoff commented as they made their way back to the main road and then out toward the highway heading north.

"She is. I couldn't have made it through everything that's happened since the accident without her." Preston sighed as the truck rocked over the road. "I just don't think she's really happy. My dad's gone a lot and she spends a lot of time alone." He fell into silence, thinking of his mother as the hum of the wheels invaded the cab. As they made the turn to head north, the mood finally shifted, and all three of them began talking about nothing and everything.

Stone smiled to himself as Preston's hand slid into his between them. "You're wearing the watch." Preston smiled at him when he saw the Christmas gift he'd given him.

Stone leaned against Preston. "And I see you're wearing your present too." He ran his hand on top of the denim fabric on Preston's legs. "I thought the Wranglers would be good for riding." Preston's hand slipped away and wound around his shoulder, pulling him closer. They'd both been surprised and pleased with the thoughtfulness of the other's Christmas gift.

The truck continued along the highway, passing through Traverse City and Charlevoix. Stone felt the fear and nervousness rise with each passing mile. His stomach began clenching, and he thought he was going to be sick. "Geoff, could you pull off?" The truck lurched and stopped. Stone opened the door and stumbled out, managing to make it to the edge of the road before losing the contents of his stomach. Still bent over and heaving, he felt a hand on his back, and as the spasms stopped, he saw Geoff standing next to him. Straightening up, he felt Geoff's arms slide around him, and he was pulled into a hug, a hand soothing his head and a soft voice in his ear. "It's okay. It'll be okay."

When Stone could move, Geoff released him, and he climbed back in the truck, and Preston hugged him close as Geoff got back in the truck. "We can turn around if that's what you want. You don't ever have to see him again," Preston murmured in his ear. "I never would have suggested this if I'd have known how it was going to make you feel."

"No. Please, Geoff, we need to get Buster," Stone pleaded, lifting his head away from Preston's chest.

"Are you sure?" Preston asked as his hands smoothed down Stone's back.

"Yes. We need to get Buster." Stone sat up, and Geoff restarted the truck, pulling back out onto the road. Stone needed to get himself under control. He hadn't thought seeing his father again would have this much of an effect on him.

"You're not alone, Stone. Geoff and I are here, and we're not going to let anything happen to you."

Stone nodded his head, but said nothing. There were so many things he was afraid of. He was pretty sure his father wasn't going to be happy to see him, and he could deal with that. Hell, he was really hoping his father wasn't home, and he could just get Buster and go. What if Uncle Pete was there? What if his father had been drinking? What if something happened to Preston or Geoff? Worry upon worry kept running through his mind, and he found his stomach starting to cramp again.

"It's okay, Stone." Preston's words were filled with concern. "I know what's bothering you, and if he's there, I'll kill him, I swear. He's never going to touch you again." Preston was holding him again, and this time, Stone let himself relax into the embrace.

As they approached town, Stone gave Geoff directions, and Stone felt the jitters start up again, but he breathed deeply and kept his nerves under control. Cresting a rise, he saw the house and barn, looking just like they always had. "The drive's just ahead."

Geoff pulled into the drive, and Stone directed him to park near the barn. "I'd like to get out of here as soon as possible." The truck stopped and they waited, but no one came out of the house or the barn. The place seemed deserted, and Stone breathed a sigh of relief. Opening the door, he stepped out and looked around. Things looked the same, but they didn't feel the same, at least not to him. This was where he'd grown up, but it didn't feel like home, not anymore. He was almost relieved—at least it wouldn't be hard to leave again.

Reaching behind the seat, he pulled out Preston's chair, unfolded it, and helped him out of the truck before pulling him backward through the snow toward the barn. He heard the door slide open, the deep rumble familiar.

"My God!" he heard Geoff mumble, and he turned Preston around, wheeling him inside.

The place smelled foul and dank. Stone looked around frantically and whistled, relieved when Buster's head poked out of his stall. Letting go of the handles of Preston's chair, he rushed to the long, brown head, stroking Buster's nose.

"Jesus Christ!" he heard Geoff exclaim from the stall door. "We need to get him out of there." Geoff swung the door open, and Stone looked inside. The floor was covered in droppings, and it looked like the stall hadn't been cleaned since he'd left. Grabbing the halter and lead from the post, he got them over Buster's nose and led him out of the stall, his hooves sloshing as he stepped. "Let's see if we can find some warm water to clean his hooves. I just hope they're still solid."

"Me too. They could rot in a mess like that." Stone looked inside the manger and water trough; both were empty. "Geoff, would you hold his lead? I'm going to get some hay and the portable trough from the trailer. Who knows when he was last fed." Stone felt his heart breaking as he raced to the trailer.

Back in the barn, he filled the trough from the hose and got a feedbag, hanging it on one of the posts. The last thing he wanted to do was put Buster back in the filthy stall, even to eat. "Don't give him too much right away," Geoff cautioned, "he may not be able to tolerate it."

"What should I do?" Preston asked.

"Over in the corner"—Stone pointed—"is a warming iron. Please bring it over, and I'll fill a bucket. We can use it to warm the water before washing him." Winter was not the best time to do this, but they had to get the stuff off his hooves so they could take a look at them.

Stone hung the feedbag, and Geoff led Buster to the food. He immediately began munching. Filling the trough, Stone set it on a bench, and Buster went for the water, drinking a huge amount. "We need to let him eat for a while and then rest before we try to transport him. He could get colic and that wouldn't help."

Stone knew that and left Geoff so he could fill the bucket from the hose. Carrying it back, he plunged in the wand and plugged it in. "I wish we had warmed the water for him to drink."

Love Means ... Freedom

"In the truck is my large Thermos. Adelle usually fills it with hot water so I can have tea. If she did, dump that in; it should take the chill off."

Stone walked into the small tack room and got a blanket, handing it to Geoff before grabbing his saddle and carrying it to the truck. After stowing the saddle in the trailer, he retrieved the Thermos, which was indeed full of hot water. Carrying it back, he poured the water into the trough, making sure to mix it with the cold. "That's better, boy."

"What the fuck do you think you're doing?!" Stone knew that voice and looked toward the door, seeing his father standing in the opening, carrying a gun. How many times had he seen him just like that? Wiry frame, his curly, out-of-control hair, jeans and a flannel shirt.

"I'm just getting my horse," Stone said levelly, walking toward his father. He was surprised at how calm he felt—actually, how little he felt, period—when he looked at this man. "Then we'll be out of here."

"I ought to shoot you for horse thieving." He tried to sound menacing, but Stone wasn't going to let him get to him. He needed to stand up to the old bastard, even though his stomach threatened to rebel again.

"A man can't steal his own property, Dad. I have the bill of sale to prove it." Stone watched as his father lowered the gun, but kept it in his hands as he strode into the barn.

"So, the queer I raised has returned," he jeered as he leaned against the stall door.

"Better a queer than a piece of shit lowlife who would kick his own son out of the house for being gay." Stone gaped as Preston wheeled himself right up to his father.

"You watch your mouth, boy!"

"Or what? You gonna hit me? That'll look real good when the sheriff gets here, you hitting a guy in a wheelchair. Your friends down

99

at the old feedbag will think you're a real man for doing that." Stone watched as Preston glared back at his father, moving closer.

Stone suppressed a smile as his father backed away. "I wouldn't touch you if my life depended upon it. Who knows what I'll catch." The man actually looked scared.

"What kind of man are you? You can't catch gayness, for God's sake." Stone watched as Preston turned in his chair. "He's your son!" Preston kept moving forward, and Stone's father kept backing away. Stone found it rewarding that the man who had intimidated him all those years was himself intimidated by a man in a wheelchair.

"He's not my son! His father is some guy his mother slept with before we were married."

Stone raced forward. "You fucking liar!" His father backed away and out of the range of his punch.

"I'm not lying, Stone. Your mother was already pregnant when I met her." The way he said it was matter-of-fact, and Stone stepped back, feeling like he'd been punched in the gut. His stomach started to roil, and he ran for the door, vomiting what little was in his stomach into the snow. Straightening up, he saw the man he'd thought was his father walking toward the house, turning around when Stone stood up. "Make sure you don't take nothing that ain't yours, or I'll call the sheriff." Turning back around, he walked up the steps and into the house, the front door closing with a thud.

"I'm sorry, Stone." Turning around he saw Preston sitting in the doorway. When he approached, Preston put his arms out, and Stone accepted the hug. "The man's an ass."

"So what if I wasn't his son, why didn't he love me? I lived with him since I was born, and after Mom died, it was only him and me." Stone felt Preston's hands slide up and down his back, soothing him.

"I can't tell you that, but whatever it was, it wasn't your fault and it wasn't something you did."

Stone pulled away. "How do you know that?"

Love Means ... Freedom

Preston pointed at the house. "Because he's the one with the problem. You're a good person who cares about other people, and he's the one that can't accept you for who you are." Preston took his hand, holding it between his. "He's the one who had years to tell you that he wasn't your father, but he waited until he knew it would hurt the most."

"How do you know it wasn't me?"

Preston swallowed. "Because I have great taste and I wouldn't be falling for you if you weren't one of the best people I've ever met." Stone looked at Preston looking for some indication that he'd heard correctly. "You heard me right."

Stone leaned down and captured Preston's lips.

"Guys, I don't think this is the time." Geoff's voice carried from deeper in the barn. "We need to get him ready to move."

Stone pulled away from Preston's lips. "Let's get done and out of here." They returned to where Geoff was standing with Buster. He'd eaten quite a bit of hay and drunk a good deal of water. "I'll get the rest of his stuff into the trailer." Stone went to the tack room and got the rest of Buster's things, loading them in the back of the truck before checking the water temperature. It was warm enough, so Stone unplugged and pulled out the heater, stowing that in the back of the truck as well before carrying the bucket to where Buster stood, happily munching his hay.

Stone bent down and gently brushed his hand down Buster's side before lifting each leg and washing away the filth. "It's all right, boy," he heard Geoff coo as he continued cleaning the legs and hooves. "How bad is it?"

Stone stood, anger filling him. "Not as bad as it could be, I suppose. They're soft in a few places, but overall the hooves are solid." This wouldn't have been an issue if he hadn't left him. A wave of guilt washed over him. He should have known; he should have come back earlier.

"Stone, it isn't your fault."

"Yes, it is." He patted Buster's forequarters. "He's my responsibility and I let him down."

"No, you didn't." Preston's voice sounded firm behind him. "He did." He saw Preston point toward the house. "Anyone who'd let an animal suffer like that isn't human."

Was this the same person he'd met a few weeks ago? He turned toward Preston, trying to figure the man out. He'd told him that he cared for him, stood up for him with his father, and even shown empathy for Buster. Stone patted a warm flank blankly. "What happened to the arrogant ass who called me Stable Boy?" he murmured almost to himself, a smirk on his face. At least he could understand that person.

"He's using it for good, like you said." Preston smirked right back.

Geoff chuckled. "Is everything ready?" Geoff asked, returning their attention to the task at hand.

"We just need to get Buster loaded, but I want to make sure his legs are dry first." Stone looked to both of them, feeling their support like arms wrapped around him. He'd been able to stand up to the old fuck for the first time. "I'll be back in a few minutes."

Stone walked toward the door. "Where are you going?" Preston asked from behind him.

"To get the last of what's mine." Without second-guessing himself, he strode across the snowy yard, stomped up the front steps, and banged on the front door.

"What do you want?" His old man's booze-soaked eyes stared back at him, framed by greasy, unwashed hair.

"The rest of my stuff, old man." He wasn't going to give him the satisfaction of calling him father, and he'd never been a dad. Stone pushed past him and entered the house, the living room messy with papers and dishes. "Still can't figure out how to take care of yourself."

Love Means ... Freedom

He didn't pause long before walking down the hall to what had been his bedroom.

He found himself pausing before opening the door, wondering what it would look like, but inside, nothing appeared to have been touched. Judging by the dust covering everything, no one had even been in here since he left. He never thought he'd be grateful for laziness.

Squatting down, he pulled a couple boxes from under the bed, checking that they were secure before stacking them near the door. Pawing through his closet, he found an old Spiderman suitcase from when he was a kid and began filling it with clothes.

"Don't be takin' nothin' that ain't yours."

Stone whirled around. "Have I ever stolen? Have I ever lied to you?" Stone kept his voice as firm as he could. "Even when you'd beat me for some imagined infraction, did I ever lie?" Stone took a step closer. "It's you who can't take the truth, old man." Stone took a deep breath, trying to calm his raging nerves, but fuck it.

He stepped toward Stone, raising an arm to strike him.

"Don't you dare." Stone held his ground, where he'd have backed away before. He held the man's gaze. "I'm not a kid anymore, and I'm certainly not your kid, or your whipping boy." He saw the man flinch. "You hit me and I'll kick your ass into next week, you useless old drunk." His voice softened as he saw the hand come down, and his anger shifted.

"I raised you and you owe me."

That was it. "I don't owe you shit!" Stone yelled. "You kicked me out with no place to go." Stone didn't even realize he was yelling.

"I know you went to Pete's. You were fine."

Stone wasn't about to be placated. "Fine! I was not fine! That perverted fuck raped me on his sofa." The shocked, disgusted look on the drunk's face was worth all the trouble. "That's right, your best friend is just as gay as I am." He hurled all the pain and hurt at the man he'd thought of as his father. The one person he should have been able to trust, and he'd found out the hard way he couldn't. Stone closed the suitcase, stacking it on the boxes. "You may be disappointed in me because I'm gay, but I'm disappointed in you as a human being. I guess that makes us even. At least I had the guts to tell you the truth." He knew he was most likely talking to a brick wall, but he was doing himself some good to get this out. Picking up the stack, he pushed the man against the doorframe as he stomped through the house and out the door.

"You okay?" Geoff took the boxes from his hands as he approached the truck. "Buster's in the back and seems remarkably happy. I think he knows he's going with you."

Geoff placed Stone's things in the back. "You ready to go home?" Geoff's eyes told him his words weren't said casually.

Stone looked to the truck where Preston waited and then back at Geoff. "Yeah." He sighed to himself. "Let's go home."

Stone got in the driver's side door, sliding across the seat so Geoff could get in too. The truck began to move out of the drive, turning onto the road. Stone managed to last until they reached the highway. By then the adrenaline had worn off, and he buried his head against Preston's chest and let the grief and loss wash over him.

Love Means ... *freedom*

CHAPTER 10

STONE felt so good leaning against him, arms around his waist, holding on for what felt like dear life. Preston could feel the shakes and gasps as he quietly sobbed against him. "It's behind you. You never have to see him again." He watched as they pulled away from the small farm, the smell of pigs finally fading in the distance. He let his fingers roam through Stone's soft hair, soothing as he comforted. "Did he hurt you?" He knew the revelation about his parentage had hurt Stone greatly, but he wanted to make sure the old drunk hadn't gotten physical. "Did he hit you?" Stone's head shook against him, and Preston continued comforting him as they picked up speed, moving down the two-lane highway.

Stone's head pulled away, and he looked up at Preston, eyes red, face flushed, and Preston continued holding him, not wanting to let him go for anything. "He didn't hit me, not to say he didn't try."

Preston felt his temper rise. "What did he do? I'll kill him, I swear." He looked deep into Stone's eyes and saw the last thing he expected: peace.

"He set me free," Stone replied after a long deliberation. "I stood up to him, really stood up to him, and the old fuck backed down."

Stone sat up, but Preston kept an arm around him. "Oh, he tried to hit me, but I threatened him right back, and the fucking coward didn't know what to do. Too bad it took me all this time to realize what a weasel he truly was. I could have saved myself a lot of pain and grief." He wiped his eyes with the back of his hand. "Did you mean what you said?" He turned to Geoff, who looked at him briefly before returning his full attention to the road. "About going home?"

"Of course."

Stone looked at Geoff in disbelief, and Preston had to admit he shared it. But he'd also come to learn that Eli and Geoff were extraordinary people with incredibly big hearts, and he had a feeling that Stone had wormed his way into theirs, just like he'd managed to worm his way into his.

"Won't Buster be cold back there?" Preston asked, concerned as saw the snow swirling around the tires reflected in one of the mirrors.

"No." Geoff answered. "He's got a blanket on, and I shut the vents so his own body heat will stay in the trailer and keep him warm. We'll stop every hour or so to make sure he's okay, just in case."

Not knowing what else to say, Preston settled on the seat and pulled Stone closer. He felt so good that he didn't want to give up the contact. Then he felt Stone return the hug, an arm worming behind him as the truck became comfortably quiet.

The miles ticked beneath the tires. They did indeed stop a few times, seeing to it that Buster was doing just fine, happily munching his hay, and by late afternoon, they were pulling into the drive and up to the barn. Preston waited in the truck while Buster and his things were unloaded. He watched as the horse was walked past the truck and through the barn doors. For a man who knew he had no patience for anything or anyone, he was surprised and astonished to find that he'd wait forever for Stone if he asked him.

The truck door opened, and Stone climbed in, starting the engine. "Is Buster settled?"

Love Means ... Freedom

"He seems at home and happy. Geoff said he'd be in soon and that he'd call the vet to take a look at his hooves in the morning." Stone drove in a large circle until they were parked near the house. "Do you have to be home at any particular time?"

"No, why?"

Stone turned off the engine and leaned closer to him, angling for a kiss. "I should have asked more clearly. Do you have to go home tonight? I was wondering if you'd stay with me?"

Preston nodded and smiled, returning Stone's kiss, hardly able to believe his ears. "Are you sure?"

Stone bit his lower lip, clearly nervous and excited at the same time. "Yes, I'm sure."

Preston looked toward the barn. "Is it okay with Geoff? It's his home, after all." And if they were going to be together, Geoff was going to have to carry him upstairs.

"When we were in the barn, I asked him if he'd object, and he just smiled at me. I think the man's related to Cupid or something." Stone looked so cute, so kissable, that he couldn't hold himself back and tugged him closer, kissing Stone hard and long before a knock at the window separated them with a start.

Sheepishly, Preston opened the door and shifted himself into the chair that Geoff had waiting, and he was wheeled backwards through the snow and into the house. "Are you sure you're okay with this?" he asked Geoff as the snow sloshed around his wheels.

"Yes. Just don't hurt him."

Preston had a denial on the tip of his tongue, but Geoff's expression said it all. He wasn't accusing, just cautioning, and being Stone's friend. "I don't intend to." That was all anyone could promise.

Inside the house, Preston stripped off his coat, and Stone zoomed him into the living room, where a football game was on the television and snacks littered the coffee table. To Preston's surprise, the person sitting on the sofa, eyes glued to the game, was Adelle, who shushed them without looking away. He and Stone joined her and cheered right along with her. Preston figured that Stone knew about as much about football as he did, but Adelle's rabid enthusiasm was catching, and Preston knew that if he wanted to keep tasting her incredible food, he needed to make her happy.

As soon as the game was over, she stood up, grabbed all the now-empty bowls, and walked into the kitchen. Preston didn't know what to say, and he looked at Stone, who simply shrugged and got up, sitting next to him. "I don't ask," he said, as Geoff, Eli, Joey, and Robbie all came into the room together. The couples all took places, sitting together. It felt so natural and accepted—no drama, no expectations, no having to be someone he wasn't.

Just as Adelle called them to dinner, Preston's phone rang. "Hi, Mom."

"Are you coming home?" She sounded a little strange.

"No." He hesitated. "Is something wrong?"

"No, honey. Are you with that young man from the farm?" Her tone changed, and she actually seemed pleased. "I'll see you in the morning."

"Okay, Mom… and thanks." It made him happy that she was pleased for him, but he had the nagging feeling that there was something going on. Shrugging slightly, he closed the phone and rolled himself into the kitchen.

GEOFF set him carefully on Stone's bed and left the room without saying anything. Having to be carried to the bedroom was about as unromantic as he could imagine, but he'd swim the English Channel for Stone. Preston found himself feeling very nervous, though. Stone had said he'd join him in a minute, and he was trying to keep his stomach from flipping out.

Love Means ... Freedom

Stone had been hurt, and hurt in a sexual way. Preston wanted to make this as wonderful for him as he could, and he only hoped he'd be good enough, could make this good enough to blot out the misery and fear he saw in the young man's eyes. It took a great deal of courage for Stone to invite him to stay, something he'd displayed a great deal of already. Movement by the door drew Preston's attention. Looking up, he saw Stone walk in and close the door behind him. "If you aren't ready, I'll understand."

Stone didn't reply right away, but he stepped closer. "When he hurt me, he took something from me that I can never get back." Stone continued moving closer until Preston could almost feel his heat through his clothes. "But I can't let him win, and if I stop myself from feeling, then he does win." Stone didn't turn or look away.

"I won't hurt you, Stone." Preston leaned forward, touching their lips together. "We don't have to do anything you aren't comfortable with, I promise." Preston's hands slid across Stone's chest, popping open a couple buttons on his shirt before slipping beneath the fabric. "You felt so good sleeping next to me—best Christmas present I ever got."

"I don't know what to do, Preston, I've only—" Preston silenced him with another gentle kiss.

"We'll learn together." Preston tugged him closer until Stone was standing between his legs.

"But you've done this before. What do you need to learn?"

Preston let his hands glide over Stone's smooth skin. "You. The only thing I want to learn is you: every curve, every muscle. The way your arm feels when it's around me; the way your leg feels when it slides against mine." Preston slipped off Stone's shirt, the fabric rustling as it dropped to the floor. "The way you shiver when I touch you here." Preston leaned forward and lightly kissed a pink nipple, feeling the small quake that rippled though Stone from head to toe. "I want to learn what your lips taste like." He kissed him again, and then

109

moved away. "What makes you pant and moan." Preston ran a hand through Stone's hair. "I want to learn every inch of you and then start over again from the beginning."

Stone's eyes had drifted shut. "I want that too."

"Then you need to tell me. Promise if there's something you like, you'll tell me, and if there's something that scares you, you'll tell me that too." He felt Stone's hand on the tail of his shirt, tugging it up, and he lifted his arms, letting Stone remove the fabric. Then their chests came together, warm skin touching and sliding. Preston found himself gasping at the heat that poured off Stone's body.

"What do I do?"

"What do you want to do?" Preston decided that he'd let Stone set the pace. Slow or fast, he was going to follow his lover's signals. His lover. Preston stopped and stared into Stone's eyes. This incredible creature with deep, expressive eyes, unruly curly hair, and the fullest lips he'd ever seen, was about to become his lover.

"Is something wrong?"

"No, everything's perfect." Preston nearly gasped as Stone took his lips in a powerful kiss, pressing him back against the mattress. More than perfect, it was spectacular. Stone's hands tentatively slid over his skin, and when a finger slid around a nipple, Preston gasped into their kiss. Everywhere Stone touched seemed hot and sensitized, as if his very skin had just gotten a taste of Stone and craved more.

His hands slid along Stone's back and down to the curve just above his butt. Preston felt Stone tense, and he backed away, splaying his hands across Stone's back. Then Stone lifted himself up and scooted both of them up to the pillows.

"I want to see you," Preston gasped between kisses. Stone backed away and looked down into his eyes before slipping back off the bed. Without replying, Stone opened his pants and let them slide down his legs. Then he opened Preston's, pulling them off and dropping them on the floor. "You're beautiful, Stone," Preston breathed as his eyes took

Love Means ... Freedom

in the vision in front of him, as his hands itched to feel. Rolling onto his side, he reached out and ran his hands over strong shoulders and down forearms. This was a man whose young body had been built through hard work, and it showed.

Preston lightly slid a hand along Stone's chest, pressing his lips to where his hands touched. He could feel Stone's legs start to shake, and he looked at his lover's face, a study in wide-eyed wonder. "Pres... ton." He let his hands slide lower, fingers gliding through a nest of curls before slipping along the perfect length. "I'm going to fall over." He could see Stone's legs shaking, and Preston smiled, knowing he'd made Stone feel so good that he could barely stand. Rolling onto his back, he made room on the bed, and Stone joined him. Their bodies entwined, legs wound together, chests pressed close, and he gasped as he felt Stone's length slide against his.

"You're driving me crazy," Preston whimpered into Stone's ear, and he lifted his head, locking their eyes together.

"What am I doing? I want to get it right so I can do it again."

"You're just being you." Stone sat up, straddling Preston's legs, cock jutting straight out, and Preston took advantage, gliding his hand over the silky smooth hardness. Stone's eyes drifted shut, his back arched, and his head lolled back, and Preston watched as the strong, lithe body above him began to shake.

With a small cry, Stone leaned forward, capturing Preston's lips in a searing kiss, their bodies mashed together. It felt almost as though Stone was trying to meld them together. Somehow, Preston managed to roll them over on the bed and found himself looking into Stone's deep eyes. He said nothing, just looked at those brown orbs staring back at him. Stone tried to bring their lips together again, but he stilled him gently and slowly lowered his lips to Stone's, capturing them, tasting them. "Stone, I know what you went through, and I can't tell you how your trust made me feel." He ran his hand through silky hair. "I'll never purposely hurt you." He leaned forward, kissing along Stone's neck

111

before sliding down his chest. The movement wasn't as smooth as he'd like, but Stone didn't seem to mind, and he made the most arousing sound deep in his throat when Preston sucked on one of his nipples.

Preston continued kissing the hot skin; chest and stomach passed beneath his lips. A surprised cry rang out as he opened his mouth and took Stone inside his mouth for the first time. The unique salty flavor he'd tasted on Stone's skin burst into his mouth as he slid his lips down the full shaft. Stone began to pull away, and Preston looked up, wondering what was wrong. "You don't have to do that."

Stone's cock slapped back against his stomach as it slipped from between Preston's lips. At first, Preston couldn't figure out if he'd done something wrong, but that little cry had told him that Stone liked it. "I want to." This must be a reaction to the things he'd done to get rides. "You taste like Heaven." He licked along the length like a popsicle, and Stone groaned. Smiling, Preston took Stone to the root, letting the head glide over his tongue as he moaned around the shaft.

Preston loved oral sex. He loved how the head felt on his tongue, the salty bitterness that filled his mouth, but most of all he loved the small sounds that went along with it, and Stone was making a symphony of those. Each and every one made Preston more and more determined to give his lover his very best. Hollowing out his cheeks, he sucked Stone back into his mouth, and the groans got louder and more urgent. He knew Stone was getting close and he sucked hard, running his tongue around the head. Stone made a muffled cry, his mouth open wide, eyes rolling back as he flooded Preston's mouth with his release, gasping for breath. Preston swallowed and slowly brought his face back to Stone's, kissing him hard and letting him taste a bit of himself on his lips.

"Preston, you didn't…." Stone flushed and began to stammer.

"I know. I wanted you to know how wonderful that can be when it's someone you care about."

"But what if I'm not very good?" He turned his head away, and Preston lightly stroked his cheek. "That's what some of the men said."

Love Means ... Freedom

Stone's eyes got watery, and Preston wanted to kick himself, but he knew he couldn't change Stone's experience; he could only replace those memories of abuse with ones of joy and caring.

"It's different when it's someone you care about." Preston had had his share of anonymous sex, and seeing Stone's expression just now was the most incredible experiences he'd ever had. He cared about him, and that made it special.

"I want to try."

"You don't have to, you know." Preston soothed Stone's hair away from his eyes.

"I want to." Stone turned them on the bed and positioned himself above Preston's cock and then stopped.

"Come here, Stone." Preston touched him beneath the chin and sat up, bringing their lips together, kissing him firmly as he petted his back. "This is making love, Stone, and nothing is required except our happiness." Preston could tell Stone was upset, and he really wanted to reassure him that it wasn't everything, that he was so much more important. Moving away, he rolled onto his stomach and turned his head to watch the expression.

Preston wasn't sure Stone would understand, but he jumped slightly as a hand slid over his back and over the curve of his butt. "I want you, Stone."

"You want me"—he heard a hard swallow—"inside you?"

"Very much."

"But won't it hurt?" Preston knew Stone was remembering his earlier experience, and he pulled him into a soft kiss.

"You won't hurt me, Stone. I promise."

"Then what do I do?"

"Use your fingers and lots of lube." Preston heard a drawer open and close, then cool fingers slid over his skin and he shivered, not from the cold, but from that soft, tentative touch that sent shivers through

113

him. Fingers that told him that this was truly Stone's first time. They fluttered over his skin before sliding between his cheeks.

The way those fingers teased and played had Preston writhing on the bed. Then a long, sleek finger circled the skin of his opening, and he moaned softly as it slipped inside him. "Is this okay?" Stone curled his finger, and Preston's eyes crossed as the zing shot through him.

"Where'd you learn to do that?" Preston whimpered as Stone massaged the spot deep within him. He thought Stone answered him, but he couldn't hear it through the haze of pleasure that surrounded him as one finger became two, scissoring within him. God, Stone was a fast learner, and Preston gave himself over to his ministrations.

The fingers slipped away and the tear of a wrapper signaled that Stone was ready. Then his lover sank slowly into him, and Preston willed himself to relax. He was entering a little fast, but Preston didn't want to say anything. Then he felt Stone deep within him, and the pleasure returned. Stone's weight on top of him, his cock filling him—it all felt so unbelievably good. "Start slow," Preston whispered, and Stone began to move. And it wasn't long until Stone was driving into him, sending Preston on a pleasurable trip to the moon.

"Stone!" Preston cried out, unable to control his errant body, and he spilled himself on the sheets under him as he felt Stone throb deep within him, making an indecipherable noise as he came. Then his body stilled, and Preston felt a warm weight settle on top of him.

"You feel so good, I don't want to move." Stone's voice in his ear made Preston smile, and he twisted his head and their lips met in a sloppy kiss. Then he felt Stone slip from his body, and Preston couldn't hold back a groan. Stone settled on the bed next to him, and Preston rolled onto his side and was drawn against Stone. "Thank you."

Preston pulled back to look in Stone's eyes. "What are you thanking me for?" He felt Stone's hand stroke his cheek, and he settled against his younger lover. "You were magnificent."

Stone stifled a yawn, and they kissed again. Stone put out the lights and climbed back into the bed, curling next to Preston. The house

Love Means ... Freedom

was quiet, the sounds of the farm surreptitiously entering the room like a rural lullaby, and soon Preston heard Stone's breathing even out and he began to snore softly against Preston's ear. Slowly, he turned, careful not to wake Stone as he watched the man sleep. With his eyes closed, lips parted just a little, he looked like an angel lying still next to him.

What could this incredible creature see in him? He was so young. Preston watched him sleep, wondering if he really had what it took to keep Stone happy. He couldn't walk, and while he was getting stronger, there were no guarantees that he'd ever be able to walk normally again. How could he saddle Stone with a cripple? He felt his throat tighten. He was falling in love with Stone, he knew it, and that scared him too. All his previous relationships had been a shambles; just look at what he'd had with Kent. Deep in his heart, he knew Kent was only interested in him for his money, or more importantly, his father's money. He'd known where he stood, and that he could deal with. But what he felt for Stone was so different, Preston didn't know how to deal with it; he only knew he needed it. The fluttery feeling in his stomach whenever Stone was near, the longing when he was away from him—he knew it meant he loved him.

Stone rolled over and scooted closer, his butt against Preston's hips, and he put his arm around him like he had on Christmas Eve, the scent of Stone's hair and skin filling his nose. Preston knew he'd give anything to have Stone in his bed and his life for years to come, but that was unlikely. Stone was just nineteen and had a lot of living to do, and a lot of things to discover about himself and the world. Preston stroked Stone's hair with his cheek. Boyfriends had come and gone, but if Stone left, Preston knew he would take a part of his heart with him. "I won't leave you, Stone." He hugged him tighter on a reflex to keep him close, but he wasn't so sure that his young lover wouldn't leave him.

"What's wrong, Preston?" Stone's sleep-filled voice reached Preston's ears, and he rolled over, burying his head against Preston's shoulder.

"Nothing's wrong. I just...." He couldn't tell Stone about his stupid fears. "It's nothing, Stone." He smoothed his hand over Stone's back, and he drifted back to sleep. To his surprise, Preston felt his fears subside. He couldn't control everything, but he'd make the most of what he had with Stone. And he sure as hell was going to redouble his efforts to walk again, because if they decided to build a relationship, he wouldn't go into it a cripple. With that resolved, the long day began to catch up with him, and Preston found his eyes lowering as sleep overtook him.

"I love you." Preston didn't open his eyes. If it was a dream, he wasn't going to wake up, and if it was real, it was a dream come true. Either way, he was happy.

"I love you too," he answered, equally unsure if he'd said the words in his dream or not.

Preston woke to Stone's warmth pressing right against him, chest to chest, and he was being hugged tightly. He tried to move away, and Stone clung tighter, his eyes never opening, a slight smile on his face. Preston relaxed and waited for Stone to wake, watching his young lover sleep as he returned the embrace.

"How long have you been watching me?" Brown eyes opened as Stone stifled a yawn.

"A while." Preston brought their lips together, and Stone pressed him back against the mattress. "Make love to me, Stone."

"Roll over." Stone whispered, but Preston shook his head.

"I want to see you this time."

"But your legs?"

Preston lifted them off the bed, wrapping them around Preston's waist. It took some concentration, but he accomplished it. Motivation was a wonderful thing. "Please, Stone." He felt a digit breach him and the rest of the world fell away. It was just the two of them, and when Stone entered him, filling him, he cried out softly, watching those big brown eyes, getting lost in them.

Love Means ... Freedom

Sighing softly, Stone settled against him, buried inside, and slowly began to move. Their bodies found a mutual rhythm, moving together as much as Preston was able. Kisses became sloppy, but as necessary as air, and their soft sounds built, becoming louder moans of pleasure as climaxes built within them both. Preston felt his body stiffen as he came between them with only the friction of Stone's body against him, and Stone followed shortly after, Preston watching his silent, open-mouthed cry, feeling Stone's body vibrate against and inside him. They lay together, comforting, catching their breath, as the house began to wake. Slowly they began to move.

After dressing, Geoff carried Preston back to his chair, and they went in to breakfast before Stone helped him to the car and drove him back to his parents'. With a kiss, Preston said goodbye and wheeled himself up the ramp and into the house. Closing the door, Preston wheeled himself toward his room. The lingering warmth and happiness lasted until he turned down the hall to see his father standing outside his door, a stern, unhappy look on his face.

CHAPTER 11

"YOU seem really happy." Joey stuck his head in the stall that Stone was finishing up. "And I know why." Joey winked as he stepped in the clean stall. "And so does the rest of the farm. You and Preston weren't particularly quiet either last night or this morning."

Stone felt his cheeks flush. "Sorry," he replied, although he didn't feel particularly sorry regarding anything about last night. In a word, it had been wonderful, and Stone felt himself blush again as he thought about it and Preston. He had no idea anything could be so magical, but seeing Preston's face when they'd joined, his eyes radiant, mouth open, the gasps, the small moans... then Stone remembered that Joey was still standing nearby and turned away to finish his work, grateful for something to do.

Joey chuckled. "It happens."

"I know. Remember, I've heard you and Robbie a few times." Stone chuckled along with Joey until they heard footsteps in the barn.

"I have the afternoon therapy class in a few minutes. I'll let you finish." Joey left the stall, and Stone finished his cleaning before moving Belle back into her fresh, clean home. Closing the door, he wandered through to the ring.

Love Means ... Freedom

"Hi, Stoney," Sherry called from where she sat on Mercury, riding around the ring. He called and waved back.

"I can't believe how far she's come." Stone turned and saw Sherry's mother, Alicia, standing next to him. "A few weeks ago she'd say nothing at all, now I can't keep her quiet." The smile on her face told Stone she was delighted.

"Has she talked about her dad?"

"Not much." Her smile faded a little. "But she will when she's ready." Her smile returned, brighter than before. "She did tell me last night that when she grows up, she's going to be pretty and she's going to marry Stoney."

"So I have a rival for your affections." Stone turned and saw Preston wheeling himself around the ring to where they stood. He was smiling, but to Stone it seemed forced and not exactly genuine.

"What are you doing here? I wasn't expecting you until your therapy session tomorrow." Stone excused himself and smiled as he walked toward Preston. "Is something wrong?"

Preston dropped the smile. "Are you almost done here?"

"Yeah." Now he was becoming very concerned, and he followed Preston back out of the ring and into the barn.

"We need to talk."

Stone could feel dread settle in the pit of his stomach. Was Preston regretting what they'd done last night? He looked carefully at his face, hoping for some sort of clue as to what happened, but he couldn't read anything. He felt certain that Preston was going to tell him he didn't want to see him anymore. "It's okay, Preston, you don't have to say anything. I understand." He began walking toward the barn door. He should have known that Preston was just being nice to him and that last night was just some sort of demented pity fuck. "You've done your good deed for the year, so you can go." How could he have been so stupid? He berated himself as he walked blindly across the yard into the house, almost collapsing as he reached the kitchen.

"What happened?" Adelle inquired, as she looked him over before pulling him to her. "What did that boy do?" He could hear the scowl in her voice as someone banged on the back door. She let him go with a pat on the shoulder, and he heard her talking at the back door. A few minutes later, she followed Preston into the room, glaring down at him. "Do you want me to stay?" She actually picked up the rolling pin she'd been using.

"No, he can say what he has to say and then go." Stone restrained himself from wiping his eyes. Adelle looked Preston over before leaving the room, glaring back at him one last time.

"Do you want to tell me what that was about?"

"You said you wanted to talk. So I figured I'd save you the trouble of breaking up with me." Stone closed his arms over his chest, like he was trying to shield his heart from Preston.

"I wasn't breaking up with you."

Stone stopped moving, and he felt himself color again. "Then what was all that about in the barn?"

"Maybe I better start at the beginning." Preston pulled a chair out from the table for Stone.

PRESTON saw his father standing in the hallway blocking his path. "We need to talk." He knew this wasn't good. His father's jaw was set and his eyes blazed with what looked like angry hurt.

"Let me get my coat off and I'll come to your office." His father nodded, and with one final glance walked toward his domain at the rear of the house. Preston shrugged off his coat and threw it on the bed, setting his small bag on the floor. "May as well get this over with." Leaving his room, he glided through the main floor, arriving at his father's office. "You rang."

Love Means ... Freedom

"Don't be flip," Milford chastised. "I have serious things to discuss."

"Okay—considering you haven't talked with me in years. At me, yes, but not with me." Preston rolled into the room. "So why don't you tell me what you want?"

"You've been home with us for about nine months, and I understand that you're making progress in therapy and should be walking soon."

"Jesus, Dad. If you get any more clinical sounding, you could be one of my doctors." Preston knew open antagonism wasn't going do any good. "I'm your son, not one of your business projects or company divisions."

"I don't treat you that way." His denial was automatic and fast.

"Yes, you do. Whenever you talk to me, you treat me like an underperforming asset that you have to develop a plan to fix or liquidate. But I'm not an asset. I'm your son!" Preston glared at his father, trying not to let his soul-deep hurt show, and he saw his father's face soften a little.

"I wanted to talk to you about your future."

"What about it? As soon as I'm out of this chair, I'll get a job and move out. You'll never have to see me again." He'd throw a party and get stark raving drunk the first day he was on his own again. Hopefully, Stone would be with him—now, that would be perfect.

"Why wait? There's an opening for a financial analyst in the Kansas City office. You're perfectly qualified."

Kansas City! Jesus Christ! "What about therapy?" Preston could feel his heart clench at the thought of moving so far away.

"They have perfectly qualified therapists in Kansas City." He sat down in the wingback chair next to him. "The bottom line is that if you're well enough to stay out all night, you're well enough to support yourself and get a job."

A denial and explanation was on the tip of his tongue, but he bit it back. His father was right. Fuck, he hated when that happened. "Okay, I'll give you that. And I agree. I should get a job." The surprised look on his father's face turned into a smile.

"So I can tell the department manager to expect you in two weeks?"

"No. I'll get a job on my own." The last thing he wanted was a job his father picked out for him, and with his father's company, no less.

Milford's eyes narrowed. "I think it best that you get away from some of the influences you've been under lately."

"Like what, Dad?" Preston was beginning to see where all this was coming from.

"I think a change of scenery might get you on the right track socially."

Preston had been right. "Dad, I'm gay. Moving across the country or around the world isn't going to change that." Preston softened his voice. "Being gay is just part of who I am. I know this is hard for you." He reached out and touched his father's hand. "But you didn't do anything to make me gay, Dad." Preston watched as his father turned toward him.

"I know that." His eyes were hard again, and he got up without saying another word and left the room.

"SO WHAT are you telling me?" Stone asked skeptically.

"That I've got two weeks to find a job or my dad will force me to take the job in Kansas City." The thought damn near made him sick, and he swallowed the bad taste in his mouth.

Love Means ... Freedom

"I'm sure that Geoff would hire you," Stone replied, looking hopefully into his eyes, and for a moment, Preston seemed to forget about everything else..

"I can't work here. I don't have anything Geoff needs." Stone reacted to his tone, and Preston huffed lightly and took his hands. "I have skills and I'll make inquiries. Who knows, I might get lucky." Stone could see that Preston was trying to put the best face on it he could.

"And if you don't, then it's good-bye Stone, hello Kansas City." He tried to keep his pain from showing, but couldn't.

"I don't want to go anywhere." Preston tugged lightly, and he bent down so he could hug him. "I want to stay here, but I may not have a choice. My father controls where I'm living, and he even controls my trust fund."

"Then what do we do?"

Stone saw the glint in Preston's eyes. "Nothing right now. Tonight I'll punch up my résumé and get some letters of inquiry out."

"What do we do now?" Stone asked as Preston tightened his hug and leaned forward, kissing him softly before teasing his tongue along his lips.

"This feels good to me." Stone's lips parted, and Preston resumed their kiss, letting his tongue explore a little. He wished he could get up those stairs and take Stone to bed so he could make love to him and show him just how much he meant to him.

"How long can you stay?" Stone returned his kiss.

"Not long enough. Jasper brought me over so I could talk to you, but this is so much better than talking."

They kissed again, and then Stone stood up. "I'll help you get to the car."

He felt Preston's hand move to his. "I don't want to go."

"I know." Stone helped Preston get out to the car and watched as the taillights dimmed in the snowy afternoon.

Adelle was waiting back in the kitchen. "Is everything okay now?"

"No." Stone felt Preston's loss.

"Did he do something?"

Stone smiled. "When he's here, I'm happy, and when he's gone, I feel lost and the doubts start again." He looked up at Adelle as he thought of Preston moving away. "Sometimes life just sucks. Just when you're happy, something happens to pull it away."

STONE sat on the sofa with Preston beside him, the two of them holding hands. "I've inquired with every company in town, banks, brokerage offices, and those that would see me all told me that I was qualified, but they weren't hiring." Preston was constantly worried and not sleeping well.

"Maybe your dad will give you more time when he sees how hard you've tried."

"I showed him all the résumés and even told him about my appointments, but he's being stubborn and says that he can't hold the position in Kansas City, and that I have to leave in a week."

"I can't believe you'll have to leave." He leaned against Preston and shifted on the sofa so he could hug him.

The door to Geoff's office opened, and he sat back up as a man stepped out with Geoff. "Would you mind if I borrowed Preston for a while?"

"No problem. I'll go check on the horses in the barn." Stone got up and saw Geoff and the other man sit down in the living room. He didn't know the man, but he carried a pile of papers and wore coveralls and a flannel shirt.

Love Means ... *Freedom*

Putting on his coat, he left the house and walked to the barn, the snow crunching under his feet. He needed to think, and he could do that best away from Preston.

Inside the barn, he checked that all the horses had hay and water before walking to Buster's stall. "I'm glad you're here." He patted the long neck before bending down to check his hooves. The soft spots had been cut away. "We'll need to take it easy for a while, but the vet says you'll be fine in a few months." He knew Buster's hooves wouldn't heal; instead, the damaged areas would need to grow out, and that would take time. "I missed you."

Buster kept eating his hay, but his ears twitched when Stone talked to him. "What am I going to do if he leaves?" Stone left the stall and returned with a brush and comb. "I love him, Buster." He began combing Buster's coat. He smiled as he realized he was pausing after each question. "Some help you are." Buster slurped some water and went back to eating, and Stone got quiet and kept working.

He didn't like the thought of Preston leaving at all. But he hated the thought of someone forcing him to even more. "His dad's keeping up the pressure, that's for sure." It just wasn't fair. He felt so helpless, and that bothered him more than anything. Stone's father had made him feel helpless, and so had Uncle Pete. Stone figured he had a decision to make. If Preston took the job in Kansas City, maybe he could go with him.

As if reading his thoughts, Buster turned his head, a big brown eye staring at him. Without thinking, Stone rested his head against Buster's body. Why was it that nothing seemed to work out for him? He liked it here. Geoff and Eli were like family—hell, they were better than his own family. They actually cared about him. Besides, it wasn't as though Preston had asked him to go along, anyway. Stone finished brushing Buster and gave him a treat before leaving the stall. He'd spent the entire time thinking and had come up with nothing at all, except that the thought of Preston leaving nearly made him ill.

Stone stopped in the tack room to put the comb and brush away, and the farm phone rang. He knew everyone else was busy. "Laughton Farms, this is Stone." He was greeted with silence and almost hung up.

"This is Milford Harding, Preston's father." He sounded like he'd been hurt, almost crying.

"I'll get him for you if you'll hang on a minute."

"No. I wanted to speak with you. Please." There was that same soft tone.

Stone almost hung up the phone, immediately suspicious, but his mother had taught him manners, and that politeness took over. "I don't know why you would."

"I assume that Preston has told you about the job in Kansas City." His voice seemed like that of a caring old friend. "He needs to take this job. I've arranged for some of the best therapists in the country to work with him. He's a brilliant financial mind, and this job will be good for him, and he's needed. There's no opportunity for him here." He sounded wounded and half-pleading.

"I know you want him to stay here with you, but he needs to use his mind and he needs to walk again. Jasper's doing a good job, but the specialists in Kansas City can work wonders for him." Stone wished that his father cared as much about him as Milford seemed to care about Preston.

"I want him to get better," Stone murmured, half to himself.

"Of course you do and so do I. But… he…." Stone heard the man choke up with concern. "Needs us to help him. I don't want him to go, either, but it's for his own benefit. And sometimes if we love someone, we have to put them ahead of ourselves." The man sounded nearly heartbroken, and Stone could feel for him even as his own heart ached in fear and loneliness at the thought of Preston leaving. "It won't be forever, but we need your help, he needs your help, to get better." Preston's father sniffed, and Stone heard him swallow hard.

Love Means ... Freedom

"I'll let you go. Please, think about what I said. It's important for him."

Stone swallowed, trying to make his throat work. "I will." He hung up the phone, his hand feeling disconnected from the rest of him. Dazed, he walked toward the house.

Hanging up his coat, Stone could hear excited voices from the living room. "If we invest the proceeds for three months, you can make an additional four percent." Preston's voice sounded so animated, like he was about to bound into the room at any minute. Stone continued to listen, but most of it was nonsense anyway. What the hell was depreciation and amortization anyway?

"They've been talking like that since you left. It's enough to make your head spin," Adelle commented softly as she opened the oven, pulling out one of her sweet potato pies, the scent filling the room.

Stone sat at the table with a cup of coffee, sinking into his own thoughts. The sounds from the other room receded, with only Preston's excited voice cutting through his thoughts.

"What's got you so quiet?" Adelle sat next to him, a hand squeezing his.

Stone pulled himself out of his woolgathering. "Did you ever let someone you loved go for their own good?" He saw a wistful look on the older woman's face.

"Lord, yes." Now she smiled, a big warm toothy grin. "I was in high school and smitten with Chad Montgomery." Her eyes got all fluid. "He was handsome and very nice to me. We met at a dance, which was really rare." Stone looked at her quizzically. "You have to understand that we're talking about the segregated South in the sixties, and he was white."

Stone nodded his rudimentary understanding, and she continued. "We used to meet on the road behind my house. He'd pick me up, and we'd drive to a fishin' hole he knew. We'd talk for hours. He used to ask me all kinds of questions, a real firebrand he was." She stopped, and Stone could tell by her eyes that she was back there, reliving the happiness.

"What happened?" Noise from the living room drifted in, and Preston's clear energetic voice reached his ears. Whatever he was doing, he sure liked it.

"His family was getting ready to send him to college, and he told me he'd take us away and move both of us north so we could be together."

"That's wonderful." Adelle's story was getting to him and he wiped his eyes.

"It was, and for a second, I considered it. But he had great things to do, and I couldn't stop him. He'd have been throwing his life away to be with me. An interracial couple then?" She shook her head slowly. "I told him he had to go and that I'd miss him." Her smile faded. "He knew I was right, and a week later he left."

"Did you see him again?"

"A few times, but from a ways away. He became a lawyer and worked hard for civil rights." She looked so proud.

"Where's he now?" Stone almost hated to ask.

She swallowed and patted his hand. "He was killed trying to help people exercise their right to vote. He did good, lots of good for lots of folks, and none of that would have happened if I hadn't let him go." She wiped her eyes and got up from the table. "That's enough of that." With a final pat of his hand, she went back to work.

"I CAN'T thank you enough, young feller." Stone jumped as he heard the man with the strong booming voice step into the kitchen. He really needed to stop his daydreaming. "You may have saved my farm. Do you really think I can do this?" He looked happier than one of Stone's father's pigs in slop.

Love Means ... Freedom

"From a financial perspective, yes, and you should be on your way to making a good profit even if prices fall." Preston glided into the kitchen, an excited flush on his face. Stone had seen that look before, and he looked away, as everyone could see him blush. "Just stick with the plan."

The man put on his work-stained coat, slipping on his boots and gloves before calling and waving a cheerful good-bye, the door banging behind him.

"Thank you, Preston. That was a big help." Geoff squeezed Preston's shoulder before walking back toward his office. Stone followed Preston into the living room, and he joined him on the sofa. He noticed that Preston was able to move from his chair to the sofa without help, but still couldn't walk. They sat for the rest of the evening, curled together quietly, with others moving in and out of the room, but Stone had no intention of leaving Preston's side.

"I have to get home." Preston gave him a kiss and then moved back to his chair.

"Tomorrow's poker night; are you going to be here?" Stone certainly hoped he'd come.

"Of course. I wouldn't miss it, and hopefully I'll have some good news that we can celebrate."

Stone felt a surge of excitement push everything else out of his mind. He loved Preston's celebrations, and his body did too.

CHAPTER 12

PRESTON pulled the new, specially equipped car into the farm's driveway, pushing the hand control down to brake. He liked that he could drive again, and his mechanic had been wonderful about outfitting the car for his use. He just had to remember to push in to accelerate, pull back to slow, and push down to brake. "I can do this." He smiled as he pulled the car to a stop. This was only his second day with the car, but he already felt freer now that he didn't have to bum rides from everyone.

The back door opened, and Stone bounded out, excited expectation on his face. "I'll help you in." Stone got Preston's chair out from the back seat, and Preston shifted into it. Stone helped him through the snow and into the house. "Did you get a job?"

"Yes, I got an offer today."

"You don't look happy about it." Some of Stone's enthusiasm waned.

Preston shrugged off his coat and Stone hung it up. "It's at the bank in Scottville."

Stone's brow knitted. "What is it? You sounded so excited yesterday."

Love Means ... Freedom

"They called and told me they were putting an offer together, and I thought it would be as a loan officer. Instead, they offered me a job as a teller. They gave me until Monday to let them know." He'd been so disappointed. He'd felt sure with his qualifications that they'd want him for something better. But it was a job. "Anyway, we can be happy that I've got a job, okay?" He reached up and touched Stone's cheek, the smooth skin sliding warmly under his fingers.

"Yeah." Stone smiled, and they made their way into the living room, where the guys were already setting up.

"Glad you could join us, Preston." Pete smiled as he thunked the chips on the table. "You in, Stone?"

"Sure, I'll play." He handed Pete a few dollars and got his chips, sitting next to Preston.

The games began, both tables talking and laughing. Throughout the evening, Preston could feel Stone's heat near him, and a few times he felt Stone's hand on his leg, squeezing softly. He swore the zipper on his jeans was going to bust open every time Stone touched him. He also swore Stone was doing it to break his concentration, because the stack of chips in front of him got smaller and smaller as the night wore on, while Stone's kept getting bigger. "You sure got the hang of this fast."

"I get the hang of lots of thing fast." Stone's hand started sliding down, and Preston had to try to help keep his poker face in place as fingers lightly ghosted over his length. "I'll raise you ten," Stone said, throwing in a chip, looking over at Preston, waiting to see what he'd do.

"I fold." Preston threw in his cards, glaring at his lover, who just winked back at him, raking in the pot.

As the evening wore on, his play became even more distracted. With every touch of Stone's hand, his stack of chips continued to dwindle. Not that he really minded. Stone seemed happy and was willing to express that happiness in the best way possible. He wasn't going to complain about a few poker hands.

The guys began leaving around eleven, with everyone helping to clean up and put things away. "Could you carry the bowls into the kitchen?" Joey asked as he passed on his way to the basement, his arms loaded with chairs.

"Sure." Preston answered, and he loaded empty bowls on his lap before gliding into the kitchen. Eli took them and loaded the dishwasher.

"Did I hear you found a job?"

"I got offered a teller position at the bank."

The dishes clinked as Eli pushed in the rack and shut the door. "Is that what you really want to do?"

"Honestly? No. But the job will allow me to stay with Stone." Eli didn't answer, and Preston turned back toward the living room to get another load and saw his lover standing in the doorway, staring at him. Preston felt himself heat under his gaze, but it soon dissipated when he saw what looked like confusion rather than passion.

"We're all cleaned up. The chairs are downstairs and the tables are put away." Joey yawned as he said his good-nights.

"Thank you all for helping." Eli smiled at them both as he ran dishwater for the rest of the cleaning. "We can vacuum in the morning." He followed Stone back into the living room.

"Are you okay?" Preston asked his unusually quiet lover.

"I will be."

"Are you ready to go up?" Geoff asked, before lifting him out of his chair and carrying him up the stairs. This was the most unromantic thing he could think of, but it got him special time with Stone, so it was more than worth it. "Soon you'll be doing this on your own." Geoff smiled at him as they reached the top of the stairs.

Love Means ... Freedom

Setting him on the edge of the bed, Geoff wished them both a good night before closing the door behind him. Preston watched as Stone moved slowly around the room, like he was stalking him. "What is it?" As an answer, his lips were taken in a bruising kiss that pushed him back on the mattress, a hand cupping his head. The kiss deepened further, stealing Preston's breath away.

Something had very definitely changed. When they'd made love previously, Stone had always been content to let Preston take the lead, but this was different... and exciting. "What do you want, Stone?" Stone took his lips again, pulling, tugging, sucking, while fingers opened the buttons on his shirt, parting the fabric and letting it fall to his sides. Shimmying slowly, Preston shifted on the bed, his head now on the pillow, his shirt on the floor.

Stone knelt next to him, his hands gliding over his skin. Everywhere Stone touched, his skin heated and zinged, but the most amazing thing was Stone's eyes. They seemed so deep, like he was being drawn into them, and he never wanted to be pulled out.

Preston loved the feel of those hands, firm and a little rough, just enough to make every nerve fire hard, threatening to overwhelm his brain. His jeans were opened and slid down his legs, the heavy fabric dropping to the floor, his belt clinking. Then he sensed those hands on his legs. On reflex, he jerked up to see what Stone was doing.

"Lay back. I know they're sensitive for you, but trust me."

He did trust Stone and he lowered his head back to the pillow. Those magic hands started at a foot, caressing his toes and sliding over the arch and heel. His calf throbbed in the best possible way when that hot palm made his muscles jump against the welcome touch.

Long, languid strokes slid from ankle to hip, making Preston sigh. Injury and months of therapeutic torture slipped away as his legs were loved. That was the only word that applied, loved. His skinny, emaciated legs were being loved. "You don't have to do that, Stone."

"Do what?" Another long stroke down one leg and up the other. "Make you feel good?" He started again, making Preston groan with the simple pleasure. "Let you know that all of you is sexy? Because you are, Pres." His voice got rough, and for a second Preston thought Stone was tearing up. "Never forget that, no matter what." The hands stopped, their heat remaining stationary before moving again. Then the hands slid away, the bed jiggling as Stone crawled off. His clothes seemed to melt away, and then he was back, kissing, petting, his warm skin pressing to Preston's. Outside, the wind picked up, whistling around the windows like it felt excluded from their love.

Stone's knees wound beneath Preston's legs, lifting them. A slender finger swirled around his entrance, teasing him before sliding inside, and Preston groaned deep and long. "Fuck...." Stone had been right; he did learn fast. The finger curled... and good.... "Stone...." The finger slipped away, followed by an exquisite stretch as their bodies joined.

"So hot... so tight," Stone groaned as he slid deep and good, Preston's lips meeting his, eyes locking again.

Preston held their lips close, kissing deep as Stone moved inside him, filling him. Then Stone's lips pulled away, and he arched above Preston, going deep, withdrawing, and going deep again. Preston's hands went to Stone's skin, sliding, caressing. Hand on his chest, he could feel Stone's heart beating, feel their hearts beating. He was going wild, all sensation heightened as a deep growl began in Stone's throat that grew to burst until he felt Stone still, the only movement now deep inside him.

Long, slender fingers wrapped around his length, stroking, teasing. His skin was so alive, the nerves so warm and close, that he was coming hard, catapulting off desire's cliff, before his conscious mind could grasp it.

Panting hard, Preston felt Stone's hands on him again, soothing, petting. Finally able to open his eyes, he saw a wide-eyed Stone

Love Means ... Freedom

watching him, then kissing him as their bodies separated, sending another shiver through him.

A cloth softly wiped him clean, and then Stone was next to him, curling close. "'Night, Pres." He curled closer, legs entwining, hips meshing, Stone's head against his shoulder, the rich musky scent of his lover combining with what was fast becoming to him the homey scent of the farm and earth that seemed to have seeped into Stone's being.

Something wet slid down his arm, just a drop. "Are you crying?" Stone didn't answer, just shook his head and kissed him, and eventually he drifted off to sleep.

Preston woke feeling chilled. "Stone." He saw him standing by the window, a silhouette against the dark and the snow falling outside. Stone turned, a blanket draped over his shoulders. "I was wondering where my cuddly furnace had gotten to."

"I'm not very sleepy right now." His voice sounded rough, like he was trying hard to hold something back.

"Did you have a nightmare?" After what had happened to his lover, Preston was sort of surprised he didn't wake screaming.

"You could call it that, I guess."

Preston watched him turn away from the window and slowly step toward the bed. "Something is wrong." It wasn't a question—Preston was vocalizing what he could almost feel in the air. "Can I help?"

"Not with this, I'm afraid." The blanket slipped from Stone's back, and his tall, slender form shone in the light that stole in from beneath the door. The covers lifted, and Stone rejoined him. Preston wondered what was wrong, and he turned on his side, pulling Stone close. At first, Stone seemed to resist, and Preston didn't know why, but eventually he cuddled back, his butt resting against Preston's hips. Something definitely wasn't right, and Preston wondered silently to himself why Stone was closing himself off. He had been so animated, so forceful in their lovemaking, and now this change puzzled him.

Soon, through his ruminations, he heard Stone's breathing even out and knew he was asleep. Now it was Preston's turn to lie awake.

He must have dozed off, because Preston woke with a start as Stone got out of bed again. "I'm sorry. I'll be back in a while."

Stone pulled on his clothes and disappeared through the door, leaving Preston alone again, staring at the ceiling. He couldn't figure out what could be bothering his lover and started to wonder if he'd inadvertently done something to hurt him, but he could think of nothing.

Unable to stay in bed any longer, Preston swung his legs over the edge of the mattress and reached for his bag near the bed. He almost overbalanced and nearly tumbled off before snagging it, and began getting dressed. By the time Stone returned, he was dressed, ready, and waiting.

"You're up." Stone looked flushed as he closed the door.

Preston patted the mattress beside him. "You want to tell me what's going on?"

Stone didn't accept the invitation; instead he paced around the room like a caged cat. Finally, he stopped, his expression hard. "I think it's best if you take the job in Kansas City."

At first Preston wasn't sure he'd heard right. Then his mind caught up, and he felt like he'd been kicked in the nuts. "What? Why?"

"I just think it's for the best, Preston." The harsh tone hurt as much as the words. "We both need to get on with our lives. You need to walk, and I need to figure out how to be on my own." Stone turned away from him. "It's for the best." Before Preston could reply, Stone had the door open. "I'm sorry." Then he was gone, the door chinking closed.

It felt as though someone sucked all the air out of the room. The insecurity and hurt he'd felt after Kent dumped him came rushing back tenfold. *I was a fool.* He really thought Stone…. *What? Loved him?* Looking at the back of the closed door, he realized he had thought that,

Love Means ... Freedom

just like he thought Kent might have loved him too. Maybe he was the biggest fool on the face of the earth to think that he could be loved. Fuck, he couldn't even walk.

The door opened slowly, and for a second his heart jumped, hoping it was Stone returning to tell him it was a joke or that this was just a nightmare and he was going to wake up any second.

It was Geoff, and Preston closed his eyes and suffered what he now saw as complete helpless indignity, allowing himself to be carried downstairs. *This is the last time I allow anything like this.* He stiffened as Geoff set him in the chair and went into the kitchen. Preston followed and looked around. Everyone looked at him quizzically, but he just shrugged and shook his head before gathering his coat and pulling it on his arms and over his shoulders.

"Thank you all for everything." Somehow Preston kept his voice from breaking.

"You don't have to go," Eli soothed as he brought food to the breakfast table. Preston almost accepted Eli's offer to join them. That man was so nice it was hard to say no to anything he asked, but he just needed to be alone.

"Yes, I do." He had no appetite, and he wanted to hide and lick his wounds.

"I'll help you." Joey got up from the table and helped him down the step and out to his car. "It'll be okay."

Preston wished he could believe that. "Did he say anything?"

Joey shook his head. "I think he went to the barn. Do you want to go see? Try to talk to him?

"No. He made his feelings very plain."

Joey opened the car door, and Preston shifted inside, throwing his bag on the passenger seat. His chair was folded and slid behind his seat. Closing the door, Preston started the engine and eased his car onto the road.

He wanted to yell, scream—fuck, he wanted to hit someone, make them hurt as bad as he did. "I didn't even say anything!" Preston pounded the steering wheel, bouncing back and forth in the seat. Pulling off the road, he shouted inside the car, screaming out his rage and hurt in nonsensical sounds that threatened to blow out the windows, until the tears came. Wiping his eyes harshly, Preston pulled himself together and pulled back onto the road, driving toward home.

As he pulled into the drive, helplessness overwhelmed him. Everything seemed beyond his control, and he didn't know what to do. Stopping the car, the feeling intensified. He had to get away from here. Pulling out his chair, he shifted into it and glided toward the door and into the house.

"Have you decided?" No preamble, just his father standing in the hallway.

Fuck it. At least he'd be away from everyone. "Tell them I'll leave on Monday." He saw the smile on his father's face. "Have someone find me a hotel room and make the arrangements." Somehow, he made it to his room without seeing the smug look on his father's face.

AFTER leaving the bedroom, Stone raced down the stairs and grabbed his coat before fleeing to the barn. He ignored the snow and the cold; nothing reached him. Crossing the yard, Stone pushed open the door and walked right to Buster's stall. His big friend looked up from his munching and turned toward Stone, bumping his chest in greeting. "No treats, sorry, boy." Stone rubbed the long nose before letting him go back to his hay, feeling more and more alone.

Stone heard voices outside and peered out from the stall door. He could see Preston getting into his car, talking to Joey before driving away. Those taillights leaving the yard were the final straw. Preston was leaving; he'd gotten what he wanted. Then why did he feel like such shit? Turning around, he draped his arms and head over Buster's back and stood there, feeling the horse's heat through his clothes.

When he knew Preston was truly gone, he patted Buster's back before closing the stall door and walking back toward the house. The sun on the snow was blindingly white, but to Stone, the world looked dull and lifeless. Opening the back door, he snuck back in the house, not seeing if anyone else was there. He simply walked through the kitchen before flopping down on the sofa. It was then he realized that the house was nearly empty, as empty as he felt.

"What happened, baby?" Adelle startled him as she sat down, taking his hand.

"I did what I had to do." Stone felt his lower lip start to tremble and he turned away, unable to look her in the eye. Putting his hands over his face, he felt himself start to tremble. Gasping for breath, he tried to keep himself together. But the harder he tried, the more his control slipped through his fingers. Finally, he completely fell apart, falling toward Adelle, who caught him in her arms and hugged him as he cried his eyes out.

CHAPTER 13

"STONE." He looked up from the cup of coffee in front of him, pulled out of the thoughts he just couldn't seem to get away from. "Eli and I are going riding. It's a beautiful day, and with the snow, the horses haven't been out much."

He watched Geoff's lips moving and hoped that he was getting everything Geoff had said. "Buster could use a ride, that's for sure. What did the vet say when he was by yesterday?" Stone found he couldn't remember shit for more than three seconds lately.

"His hooves are almost back to normal, and the vet said some light exercise would be good." Geoff put a hand on his shoulder, and for a second, Stone let himself imagine that it was Preston's.

"He'd love to get out." Stone stood and poured the coffee down the sink, setting his cup in the drain.

"And you need to do something to get your mind off Preston," Geoff scolded lightly, knowing that Stone was still hurting.

The denial was on the tip of his tongue, but he knew Geoff wouldn't believe it and simply nodded his head. "I guess so." He looked Geoff in the eye. "I know I did the right thing, and yet I still feel like a total shit!"

Love Means ... Freedom

"That's probably because your head is telling you one thing and your heart is telling you another. You need to get your mind off it and think about yourself and Buster for a while." Geoff threw Stone his coat and grabbed his own. "Come on, there's nothing better for thinking than taking a ride." Geoff slid his coat over his arms, and Stone finally started to move, pulling on his own coat and grabbing a hat and gloves before leaving the house. It might have been sunny outside, but he knew it was still cold.

In the barn, Eli was already brushing Dusty, and when Stone opened Buster's stall to greet his friend, he saw him brushed, saddled, and ready for their ride. He swallowed hard at Eli's thoughtfulness. Fuck, he'd been emotional lately. Leading Buster out of the stall, he met Geoff and Eli in front of the barn. "We need to be careful, but if we keep to the clear areas, we should be fine." Geoff gracefully mounted his midnight black stallion. "We can't stay out too long in this cold." Geoff started his horse forward and led the way out of the drive and onto the side of the road. Stone would have liked to be able to ride across one of the fields, but that was too dangerous. Holes couldn't be seen, and the deep snow would bother his horse's legs and hooves.

"Lead the way and we'll follow," Eli called back to Geoff, and Stone started Buster walking forward, his mount's head bobbing excitedly.

"You're glad to be out, aren't you?" He patted the long, warm neck as they moved onto the area beside the road.

The pine forest around the college provided an oasis of green in an otherwise white landscape. Fields of pristine white stretched from the road on the other side back to the windbreak trees that formed the border in the distance. "It's so bleakly beautiful," he said to himself as he rode. The crisp air and the quiet clomp of hooves lulled him into a peaceful place he hadn't felt in a while. This truly was what he needed. "You okay, boy?" He listened carefully to Buster's hooves for anything unusual, concentrating on his gait, making sure he wasn't in any discomfort. It didn't seem he was. Buster's head was high, and he almost pranced with an excitement that seemed to transfer to Stone.

Since Preston had left a little over a month earlier, he hadn't been excited about anything except working with Sherry and the kids. She had wormed her way into his heart, and every time she called him Stoney, he could feel himself melt. Other than that, he didn't seem to give a rat's ass about much of anything.

"Stone!" Geoff called, and he waved him forward, slowing his horse until they were riding side by side down the nearly deserted country road. "I've been worried about you."

Stone felt his head lower a little. "I know. I'm sorry."

"There's nothing to be sorry for. I'm just concerned, and so is everyone else." The clomping of hooves was the only sound breaking the silence as Stone felt himself retreating again. "Do you want to tell me what happened? You two seemed so happy."

"Nothing happened, really." Stone really didn't want to talk about this, but Geoff's eyes prodded him. "I just thought he'd be better off doing what he loved." He turned away before finding his gaze drawn back to Geoff. "Here he could only get a job as a bank teller. There he could do what he did for that farmer." Stone felt a cold wetness on his cheek, and he brushed it away quickly. "I couldn't hold him back." Stone kicked Buster gently, and he sped up, moving them both to the front and effectively cutting off further conversation. He did not want to talk about this.

"I did what was right," he mumbled to himself. "I did what I had to do for Preston."

"If you keep telling yourself that...." He started when Geoff drew up beside him. "You might begin to believe it." Then Geoff spurred his black stallion on, taking the lead once again. Stone breathed a sigh of relief until Eli drew alongside him. *What was this, musical horses?*

"He's only concerned."

Love Means ... Freedom

"I know. I just can't talk about it, not yet." Stone forced himself to look at Eli.

"It's not good to keep it bottled up." Eli smiled at him, his eyes bright. "We'll be here when you're ready, and we promise to listen, and only listen."

The talking subsided as a car passed, giving them a wide berth, and slowly his melancholy feelings began to recede again as the cool, crisp air cleared his head. Geoff crossed the road, turning them back toward the farm, and Stone felt Buster slow, like he was reluctant to return. "It's okay, boy. I promise we'll do this more often," Stone soothed. Crossing the road again, they rode into the barnyard and dismounted, each leading his mount into the warm barn.

In his stall, Buster impatiently let Stone remove his bridle before going right to his manger to eat. Stone loosened the girth and slipped off the saddle and blanket, steam and heat rising from the horse's back.

"Out for a ride?"

Stone knew that voice well. "I went with Geoff and Eli." He carried the saddle and blanket past Jasper. "Would you close the stall?" Stone walked past, and Jasper shut the door, following him to the tack room.

"Have you heard from Preston since he left?"

Stone shook his head slowly. Preston hadn't called him at all. Not that he should have expected it, but he was curious how he was doing, and if he was happy and liked his new job. Stone hadn't called him, either, figuring Preston was probably upset with him.

"What happened, anyway?"

Was today pester-Stone-about-Preston day? "Hasn't Preston told you?" He put the saddle on its perch and hung up the rest of the tack.

"All he said was that you wanted him gone and told him he should take the job in Kansas City." He heard Jasper sigh. "You broke his heart."

Stone momentarily stopped working, his stomach twisting with pangs of guilt. "I did what was best, what I had to do," he repeated to himself. *Fucking hell.* "I broke my own too," he mumbled, before grabbing the saddle for one of the ponies. "I have to get things ready for a riding session." Stone hurried out of the tack room and away from Jasper, hurrying down the aisle and into one of the stalls before dropping the saddle on the bedding and sliding down the wall. He'd hoped it would get easier, but it hadn't. Every day it got harder, and he missed Preston more and more.

Mercury turned around and eyed him warily before returning to his food. "Fuck, fuck, fuck!" He pounded the stall door before covering his eyes with his hands. He had to stop this. His work was suffering, and he hated feeling this way. Forcing himself to stand, he picked up the saddle and got Mercury ready for the rider.

Keeping his mind from wandering, Stone got the other ponies ready for their riders, and as the kids arrived, he heard a now familiar, happy voice. "Stoney!" He stepped out of the stall, and Sherry raced to him, throwing her arms around his neck. "I missed you."

"I missed you too." Stone set her down.

"Look what Mama bought me." She stepped back and pulled up the legs of her jeans. "Red boots!" Her face was all smiles.

Stone laughed as she pranced happily around the barn. "Just like a real cowgirl." Stone watched her dance happily. "Are you ready?"

"Yup." He led her to Mercury's stall, and she took the reins and walked him toward the ring, just as happy and proud as she could be. "Will you help me get on?"

"Once you're in the ring." He followed behind along with Sherry's mother, both of them smiling and wiping their eyes at the same time, but for different reasons.

Stone helped Sherry mount, and for the next hour, he worked with the young kids. Some of them, like Sherry, had responded well to the therapy, and the class had become louder, happier, with more chatter, giggles, and outright fun. A few of the boys were still very quiet, and Stone worked with them, giving them the extra attention he hoped they needed.

"You're amazing with them," Jasper commented at his shoulder as they stood at the rail, watching the kids. The ponies knew what to do, though some of the adventurous kids had even learned to steer and were starting to control their ponies.

"Thanks." Stone didn't know what else to say and stood quietly watching the kids as Eli and Joey wandered around the ring, helping the riders.

At the end of the session, Stone got the horses settled, and Sherry found him, giving him a goodbye hug. When the horses were settled in their stalls again, Stone walked back to the house.

He found Adelle working in the kitchen. Stone dodged her hand as he snagged one of her chocolate chip cookies before wandering into the other room, where Robbie sat in a chair, reading with his fingers,

"Is that you, Stone?" He closed the thick book.

"How do you always know?"

Robbie smiled. "Did you and Sherry have a good session?"

"Okay, this is getting weird."

Robbie began to laugh, "In addition to keeping the schedule, I noticed that when you're happy, you step lighter and a little faster, and lately the only time you do it is after Sherry's wrapped her Stoney around her little finger." Robbie raised and wagged his pinky in his direction, laughing at him. "So you want to tell me about it?"

"What is it with everyone today?" Stone flopped down onto the sofa, the springs squeaking, his laughter dying.

"I can't speak for everyone, but I for one note that since Preston's been gone, you can chill a room faster than the north wind." Robbie put down his book. "And this southern magnolia can't take much more cold. So I figure that until you get over whatever you got in your craw, spring isn't going to come, and I've been shivering since October."

"Amen," Adelle echoed from the kitchen.

Robbie sat back in the chair. "So spill it. What happened with you and Preston?"

Stone looked toward the kitchen and sighed before telling Robbie what he'd done, how he'd let Preston go for his own good.

Robbie rolled his eyes, which nearly freaked Stone out. "We have a saying in the south: 'Get off the cross because someone else needs the wood'."

"What the hell does that mean?"

Robbie ignored the question. "You decided that Preston would be better off away from you after he spent almost two weeks trying to find a job so he could stay."

"I guess."

"Well, that's a steaming pile of shit." Stone gulped and did a double take. He'd never heard Robbie speak like that. "You can tell yourself that all you like, but I think you were scared. You figured Preston would stay, and you were afraid he'd realize you weren't who he wanted and that he'd leave you. So instead of giving it a try, you pushed him away and convinced yourself it was for his own good."

"That's not true!" Stone leapt from the sofa. "He was so happy when he was helping that man with his finances, and he'd never be that happy working as a bank teller."

"Relax, Stone. I'm here to help, remember." Stone sat back down, still feeling like he wanted to bolt, and Robbie continued. "Yes, he was excited when they were working together, but he was happiest whenever he was with you."

"How could you tell?"

Robbie glared at him, obviously annoyed. "I may be blind, but I'm not stupid." Robbie's voice softened. "I could hear it in his voice and in his laugh. He loved you, Stone, and you threw it away without asking him what he wanted. Did you ever think that he may have been perfectly happy working as a bank teller if he had you to come home to?"

Stone felt his throat start to close and his stomach cramp. "Oh God." The tears started, and he put his hands over his face. "It's true. I pushed him away." He felt Robbie's arms around him, hugging him tight, as he realized what a fool he'd been. "I loved him, Robbie, and I never told him." The tears began in earnest. "What am I going to do? I miss him more every day." Once the dam burst, he couldn't control the tears, and they flowed freely.

"I know." Robbie rocked him slowly. "I know. I felt the same way when I had to leave after I met Joey. Each day apart felt longer that the last, and I felt more and more alone."

"What happened?" Stone raised his head, tears streaking his cheeks.

"Joey came to visit and showed me just how much he loved me. When he was about to leave, he asked me to come back with him."

"What should I do?" Stone wiped his eyes, feeling like a little girl as he tried to control his tears.

"I can't answer that for you." He let himself be pulled back into a hug. "That's something you need to decide, but I can tell you that this time, whatever you do, you need to listen to your heart. It won't steer you wrong, I can promise you that."

CHAPTER 14

"PRESTON, could you come in here?" He cringed, grateful he couldn't be seen.

Preston hung up the phone he'd answered seconds ago. Looking toward the door, he debated using the new walker, but from the irritated tone of his supervisor's voice, he figured speed would be better. Transferring himself to the wheelchair, he grabbed a pad from his desk, setting it on his lap, and glided across the carpeted floor.

"What is this?" The man held up the report Preston had spent days compiling.

"The second-quarter projections you asked for," he answered levelly, wheeling himself to the small table against the office wall.

"I asked for the first-quarter projections!" The man's face turned deep red.

Preston held his temper, knowing that the man had asked for the second-quarter projections. He'd spent most of the weekend in the office working on them, mainly because the first-quarter projections had to be completed first. Preston reached to the messy desk and pulled out a nearly identical report. "You mean this?" He handed him the

Love Means ... Freedom

report and left the office without another word. The man was such an ass.

Back in his small office, Preston had only just settled behind his desk when the phone rang again.

"We need to review these figures."

Preston shook his head. The man's office was one away from his, and he still always used the phone—for everything. You'd think *he* was the one who had trouble walking, the walrus. "Then come down here and I'll review them with you." Preston's arms were tired and his legs ached from the hours of therapy. He heard sputtering through the phone, but ignored it. The man did his best to make Preston's life as hard as possible.

"Just because your father...."

Blah, blah, blah. Preston hung up when the man finally stopped yammering.

Preston loved the actual work he was doing. The division had been performing poorly, and through hard work, Preston had been able to help identify the issue. For the first time he could remember, his father had actually been pleased, but that only made things worse between him and his superior, who now thought Preston was after his job.

Preston spent the next hour reviewing all the figures and what was behind each one. "It should be easier next time because I built the logic into the spreadsheets."

Finally, the man left, and Preston saw by his watch that it was almost time to leave. As he was finishing up, his cell phone vibrated on his hip. For a second, he hoped it was Stone, but he'd pretty much given any hope Stone would call.

"Hi, Jasper."

"Hey, Preston. Just called to see how you're doing."

"As well as can be expected. I'm using the walker as much as possible, but it's not easy here in the office." That was the one good thing happening recently—he'd been able to get out of the chair and actually walk. "The work's okay, and it's already spring here. The grass is starting to green up, and there's even a few early flowers peeking through." He never passed up the opportunity to rub in the warmer weather.

"Ass. It snowed here again last night." Jasper laughed. "So how are things really?"

"Honestly?"

"Yeah, that's why I asked."

Preston lowered his voice. "My boss is a lazy fuck, few people talk to me because I'm the owner's son, and there's nothing to do around here. I don't know anyone, and I hate living here." Preston fidgeted with a pen on the desk. "I like the work, though."

Jasper laughed loudly. "At least you're not bitter."

Preston couldn't help joining in his laughter. Jasper had always been able to make him feel better.

"I saw Stone today."

Preston's momentary lightheartedness faded, and he felt a familiar stab in his heart.

"He looked miserable."

"Good. He deserves it." He knew it was a petty thing to say, and it didn't make him feel any better anyway.

"I think he misses you."

Preston felt his head begin to throb. "Can we talk about something else? I spend enough time wondering what the hell happened."

"Okay, fine." Jasper sounded annoyed. "How's your therapy coming?"

Love Means ... Freedom

"It's okay. I miss you, though. The therapist is a real sadist. Just like you—but he doesn't make me laugh."

"That's because he doesn't have my fabulousness!" Jasper sang into the phone.

Preston found himself smiling again. "That's it exactly." He wished Jasper could see him rolling his eyes. The happiness died away and both sides of the line became quiet.

"Pres."

He knew that tone, and something was coming. "Please call him. You're miserable missing him and he's missing you."

The anger began to build. "He threw me away, Jasper, just like Kent. He told me to leave and take this job. He couldn't have made himself plainer."

"Don't paint Stone and Kent with the same brush. That loser Kent never cared for you."

"I'm not sure Stone did, either," Preston replied halfheartedly, not truly believing it himself. *How could Stone have faked the look on his face when they'd been together?*

"What happened before he asked you to go?" Jasper's voice was soothingly soft, and Preston felt himself falling for it, just like Jasper knew he would. *Damn it.*

"We made love." There, he'd said it out loud. "He touched my legs, Jasper, made me feel whole again." He sniffed loudly. "When we were together that last time, he made me forget for a while. I really thought he loved me." Preston swallowed around the lump in his throat.

"There's one way to find out. Call him."

"No way!" He couldn't bear to be rejected again.

"You're a stubborn ass, you know that? Your arrogant ego won't let you make the first move," Jasper chided. "Damn it, Pres, he loves you."

"He's got a strange way of showing it." His heart beat a little faster anyway, belying his own words.

"Let me ask you this; if he calls, will you at least talk to him?"

"If he calls." Preston had had enough of this conversation and said good-bye before hanging up the phone, getting back to work.

Finishing up, Preston packed up for the night, gathering his things and gliding toward the elevator. He met a few people, who said good night and hurried on their way without stopping.

In the parking lot, he unlocked his car and got inside, getting everything put away before driving home. Home—that was a joke. His tiny apartment didn't feel like home, never would. It was only a place to eat and sleep.

Pulling into his parking space, he got out and grabbed the walker from the back seat, making his way to the elevator and then up to the apartment. It had come furnished and everything was impersonal, industrial, and definitely not comfortable.

Preston spent the evening like he did most: sitting in front of the television and working on reports or putting together divisional revenue statistics.

Yawning with relief, he turned off the television, put his dishes in the sink, and got ready for bed.

Beneath the scratchy sheets, he tossed and turned, hating the way the industrially starched linens felt on his skin. Nothing felt right, sounded right, or smelled right. "I want to go home." Preston let his mind wander, and images of the barns and farmhouse filled his mind. Belle walking around the ring, even Stone's indignant expression when he'd called him Stable Boy.

"Fuck." Preston sat up in bed. That wasn't his home. But try as he might, when he thought of home, he thought of the farm and Stone, not his parent's big, fancy house on Lakeshore Drive. "Stop it," he said to the empty room, pounding his pillow with his hand, trying to get himself to settle.

Love Means ... Freedom

Turning on the light, he reached to the nightstand for his phone and began dialing, but stopped his fingers before pressing the last number. What the hell was he doing? Stone had sent him away; he didn't want him. He was sure Jasper meant well, but he knew where he stood with Stone, and it was over and time for him to move on. Putting the phone back, he turned off the light and prepared for another sleepless night.

Preston couldn't get comfortable, shifting from his side to his back to his stomach. Finally, he fell asleep only to hear Stone's voice telling him he was sorry.

Jerking awake, he rubbed his eyes and looked around the dark room, listening. Nothing. Everything was quiet. He could have sworn Stone's voice had been real. "Now I'm hearing things." Relaxing back on the bed, he figured he must have dreamed it. Maybe Jasper was right, maybe he had to talk to Stone, ask him why? If nothing else, he'd have some sort of closure and could move on. With that decision, something deep inside unknotted. His mind finally let go of the worry, hurt, and angst that had plagued him for weeks. Scratchy sheets or not, the rigid tension in his muscles melted away and he slept—finally, restfully, slept.

The buzzing in his ear wouldn't stop. Pulling the pillow around his head, he tried to shut it out. Slapping the alarm, Preston groaned as he forced himself to wake. After weeks of insomnia, he'd slept, and his body ached for more. Grinding his eyes open, the stark walls and drab furniture were enough to make him close them again.

Sighing audibly, he got up and used his walker to get to the bathroom, his body protesting every move as though it didn't want to go into work, either.

Dressed and cleaned up, Preston got ready to leave and noticed the red blinking light on the answering machine. Pressing the play button, he heard Stone's recorded voice come from the machine. "I'm sorry, Preston. I miss you so much. Please call me." Sniffles and small sobs accompanied the message; an image of tears running down Stone's face flashed into his mind, and he felt his heart leaping at the glimmer of hope. The hurt and anger he'd been nursing for the last month threatened to bubble to the surface again. Unsure of what to do, Preston turned and left the apartment, making his way to the elevator.

"PRESTON!"

He looked up in surprise to see the walrus standing in his doorway, looking very impatient. "Are you listening?"

"I was preoccupied. I'm sorry." He tried to look contrite, but probably failed, because he really didn't care about this lazy man's opinion.

The walrus made no effort to hide his annoyance. "I was asking you if the revenue statistics for the fiscal year were done."

Preston fished on his desk, finding the stack of papers he wanted. The man insisted he get everything on paper. Preston could have e-mailed the report last night, but he wouldn't have looked at it anyway. "Finished them last night." He held them up, offering them to his boss. "I made some improvements to the form we were using. If you want to review them, we can." Not that the man was likely to understand them anyway.

The walrus snatched the papers from Preston's hand, and he pulled his hand away, getting a paper cut that stung. "Damn it." Sucking on his thumb, Preston grabbed a napkin to wipe up the blood and found his mind drifting again. "That damn message," he mumbled without heat to himself as he threw the bloody paper in the trash. How could so few words cause so much confusion?

Steadying himself, he checked his watch and pulled out his phone, dialing without the hesitation of last night. The phone rang and rang. Preston was ready for it to flip to voice mail. "Hello, Preston?" Stone sounded small and scared.

Love Means ... *freedom*

Preston's heart leapt just hearing his voice. "Yes, it's me. I heard your message." The line went silent. "Are you still there?"

"Yes." It sounded like Stone was crying. "I'm so sorry, Preston." The line went dead.

He stared at the phone wondering what had happened. Huffing, he began dialing Stone's number when his desk phone rang. Irritated, he closed his cell and answered the phone before gathering his things and using his walker to go to his boss's office, grabbing the cell phone from his desk.

DAMN, that meeting had taken forever, and the entire time, he'd kept hoping Stone would call back, but his phone hadn't rung. Flopping in his chair, he rubbed his tired legs and tried to get back to work, but found himself staring at the phone. "Fuck." Picking it up, he dialed, but it went right to voice mail. Hanging up without leaving a message, Preston began to worry. What had Stone been sorry for? In his message, he said he missed him. That memory made his heart race, and he tried not to let himself get too excited, but he couldn't help it.

Finally, the phone vibrated on his desk. Recognizing the number for the farm, he answered it. "Preston, it's Geoff."

"What's wrong? Is Stone okay?" The questions poured out frantically.

"Stone ran out of the house a while ago, really upset. We found him in the barn. We think he must have startled Buster, and the horse kicked him. He's on his way to the hospital."

Preston's heart almost stopped right there. "Is he going to be okay?"

"I don't know. He wasn't conscious when I saw them putting him in the ambulance. I'm leaving for the hospital now." He could hear Eli calling behind him that the ambulance was ready to go and that they

155

were going to follow it. "I've got to go." Geoff hung up, and Preston closed the phone, staring at it.

Finally deciding what he needed to do, Preston dialed again. "Mom, I need your help." He explained what had happened. "I know you and Dad don't understand, but I need to do this."

He could almost see the expression on her face. "Your father and I don't always see eye to eye. I'll make some calls and see what I can do."

"Thanks, Mom." He hung up and tried to go back to work. There were things he needed to finish up.

An hour later, his phone rang again. "Ramon got what you needed." The man was the god of travel agents.

"He won't tell Dad, will he?"

"Of course not." She sounded offended for him. "Here's the information." Preston wrote it down.

"You're a life saver, Mom."

She was quiet for a while. "You really like this young man, don't you?"

"Yeah, I do." He had to be honest with her and himself.

"Then why did you take the job?" He waited. "Forget I asked. I know your father means well, but the man can be a stubborn ass sometimes... I guess it runs in the family." They said good-bye and hung up. *Now to face the walrus.*

CHAPTER 15

STONE floated happily, his eyes cracking open: a dim room, warmth, soft noises, only calm movement. His eyes felt so heavy. He tried to look around, but was too tired. Letting his eyes drift closed, he fell back into the happy, floaty abyss. This time he dreamed. Buster was there, bumping his chest and looking for treats. "It's okay, boy, I know you didn't mean it." He rubbed the long nose and felt an arm around his waist, Preston's smooth cologne tickling his nose. Turning in the arms, Preston pulled him close, standing in front of him, kissing him. This was definitely a dream, and he went with it, letting it float over him like a security blanket.

Beep... beep... beep—a sound entered his dream, jarring it, stopping the fun and perfection. Beep... beep... beep. The illusion faded away, and he became aware of voices, real voices, coming from nearby.

He tried to open his eyes, but they felt full of sand. Swallowing gently, his dry throat ground and pain shot through him. He groaned a little, and the voices stopped.

"Sweety, here's some ice." He saw movement and something cold slid between his lips, and icy water glided down his throat, soothing the pain away

"Where am I?" Stone tried to look, but his eyes felt heavy and drifted closed again.

"In the hospital, honey, you hit your head."

"Buster."

"He spooked and kicked you." That explained why his chest felt like he'd gone nine rounds. The voice was reassuringly familiar, even if he couldn't place it right now. "You fell and hit your head on the stall."

"Hmm."

A hand slid into his, another caressing his arm. "We were so worried."

Slowly, he rolled his head toward the second voice and saw Robbie standing next to him. He squeezed his hand, and Robbie smiled at him, his hand continuing to caress his skin. Looking around the room he began to focus. Geoff stood near his feet with Eli next to him, both watching, looking concerned.

"You're going to be okay." Turning his head the other way, he saw Joey, who lifted a cup and placed a straw to his lips. Sipping a little, he swallowed and spilled on himself. Joey dabbed at him with a tissue before putting the cup down again.

"How long?"

"You've been here since yesterday." Geoff, that was Geoff's voice he'd heard. "You had us frantic, but you're going to be fine." Someone squeezed his other hand. "We'll be here if you need us." Stone nodded a little. "Rest." He let his eyes close.

Stone was aware of people leaving. Robbie and Joey said good-bye. He vaguely heard Len and Chris stopping in, and felt what he assumed were their hands squeezing his. He opened his eyes and saw the two older men smiling at him, obviously relieved. Stone tried to talk, but just felt too tired, squeezing their hands again before closing his eyes. This time the world fell away, and he dreamed again, disjointed, garbled things that made no sense. He kept dreaming he was swimming toward an island and he could see Preston on the beach. The water was warm and he swam, getting excited as he got closer. But whenever he got close, the island moved farther away. "Preston, Preston," he called as he got farther and farther away.

"It's okay." Stone felt a hand on his, and he opened his eyes, looking around the room. Geoff sat in the chair next to his bed, with Eli nearby. "You were just dreaming." Stone's eyes darted all around the room until he remembered where he was. "You're okay, and we're not leaving you alone. Do you need anything? Are you in pain?"

"Head hurts. Chest hurts." That was all he could say, because each breath made it feel like someone had been dancing on top of him.

"I'll get the nurse to get you something, and I ordered you dinner. It should be up soon." Geoff pressed the button, and someone came in, asking him about his pain and wanting him to give them a number or some such nonsense. It fucking hurt, and she finally put something in his IV and the pain began to subside. Food arrived, and Geoff fed him a few bites of the awful stuff.

"Adelle?"

"She said she'd be up later to see you."

"Bring food." Whatever Geoff was giving him felt like glue and tasted worse.

"I'll be sure to tell her." Geoff gave him a bite of something sweet and chocolaty, and he ate it, asking for more. He managed about eight bites and then closed his eyes again. Belly full, body tired, he slept, sort of.

Someone came in and left again, but the pain meds had kicked in and he didn't really care. That floaty feeling was back and it felt so good, and the dreams were back. Preston was here with him, sitting next to him. He could almost feel his fingers stroking his hair, Preston's hand in his. "Preston." He wanted so badly for it to be real.

His dream-Preston spoke to him this time. "I'm here, Stone."

"I'm sorry, Preston. Don't go again." He held on to his dream-Preston just like he wanted to hold on to the real one. "I made you go and I'm sorry." The dream faded and his mind quieted.

Light coming through the windows woke him, along with the tightness from his chest. Opening his eyes, he saw the drab ceiling and the blank television clearly. He was still tired, but his vision and mind were clear. Turning his head, he saw someone curled in the chair next to him, a blanket over his shoulders, head turned toward the wall. "Geoff, you should have gone home."

The head turned and it wasn't Geoff. "I'm here, Stone."

Preston's eyes looked back at him from the chair. "How long have you been here?" Stone asked, barely able to believe his eyes.

"Got here last night. I told Geoff I'd sit with you, and he went home for a while." That smile he loved shone back at him, and Stone blinked to make sure he wasn't seeing things.

"You're really here?" A hand slid into his, and at that moment, Stone knew for sure it was real.

"I'm really here."

"I'm sorry, Preston. I was scared and thought you'd be better off, and I wanted you to be happy and…."

One of Preston's hands stopped his blathering with a gentle touch to his lips. "We'll talk later. You need to rest and get better."

Stone wanted to tell Preston so much. How much he missed him, how bad he felt. How stupid he'd been for telling him to take that job. Instead, he breathed a sigh of relief that at least Preston was here now and holding his hand. "How long are you staying here?"

"I don't know, Stone."

"Oh." He swallowed, and the pain in his throat started up again. Reaching for the water on his tray, he took a small sip, setting the cup back down and looking over at Preston.

Love Means ... Freedom

"It depends, but I'll be here for a few days at least." Preston didn't withdraw his hand, and Stone took that as a good sign even if he didn't tell him he was back to stay for good. He felt so guilty that he figured he'd take what he could get. "The nurse said that you should be able to go home in a day or so."

As if on cue, a nurse entered the room. "Are you feeling better today?"

"Yes." He watched as she messed with the tubes.

"Are you in pain?"

"Not really. My chest aches, but not as bad as yesterday, and the headache seems to be gone."

She smiled at him. "That's good." She fiddled with the IV some more, and then took off the bag and began removing the tape from his arm. "We're going to pull this out and then get you some breakfast."

"Is it that same stuff I had yesterday? 'Cause if it is, I'd rather starve." He smiled at her, and she smiled back.

"Now I know you're feeling better, if you can make fun of the food. That's the signal that you're almost ready to go home." He felt slight prickles of pain as she removed the needle and then bandaged his arm with a practiced ease and gentle touch. "There, all done." She handed him a card. "Here's a menu; order what you like. Just dial 3250 and they'll have it sent up." She went to her computer on a cart and started typing before leaving the room.

"Would you like me to help you?" Preston took the card and began running down the offerings. Together they ordered what they thought would be the things least likely to be shoe leather and placed the order.

"Preston, I…."

"It's okay, Stone. I had a talk with Robbie just after I got here. He told me what you told him." He felt Preston hold his hand again. "I won't go anywhere until you can come home, so just relax and get better. Sleep, if you like. I'll be here." Preston's hand slipped away, and Stone watched him get up and unfold a walker before making his way to the bathroom.

"You're walking!"

"With this thing? Yeah."

"Who cares, you're walking all on your own." Stone shifted on the bed and watched as Preston opened the bathroom door. "And you're wearing your Wranglers."

Preston stopped and looked over his shoulder. "Are you looking at my butt?"

Stone lowered his eyes. "Uh-huh. I never got to see it before, not like this. You look good in the jeans." He did, too, those jeans hugging that tight, round butt. Stone looked away because he was getting excited, and the sheets were so thin you could see everything through them. And to top it off, they had him in one of those gowns that didn't hide anything. Maybe someone would bring him something decent to wear if he asked.

The food arrived, and Stone took a few bites while Preston finished up. His stomach wasn't so sure how it wanted to react until he started eating, and then it seemed to remember that it was empty and his appetite kicked in. Preston came out of the bathroom and sat back in the chair. "You want some? I'll share."

Stone ate what he could and Preston finished off the rest. It wasn't half bad, and with his stomach full, Stone's eyes began to get heavy again and he dozed off, only to be awakened by the doctor, who pulled the curtain and lowered the blankets before feeling around. "Looks like you were really lucky. There's lots of bruising, but no broken ribs. You have a concussion, though, so we'll keep you around for a day or two just to be sure." His cold hands pressed at Stone's side, making him jump. "Does that hurt?"

"No. Just cold hands."

Love Means ... Freedom

The doctor nodded and pulled the blankets back up before pushing back the curtain. "I'll see you tomorrow. Just rest, and you ring for the nurse if your vision gets blurry or your ears ring." He made some notes and left the room.

Stone yawned and let his eyes drift closed again. This time when he woke, Joey and Robbie were sitting on the sofa thing under the window, talking softly. "Your lunch should be here soon," Joey informed him. "We're going to take Preston down to the cafeteria for a while, but we'll be back."

"I'll be here." Stone watched as Preston got up and slowly left the room, using the walker. His lunch arrived awhile later, and he ate while he watched television. The guys returned, and they spent the afternoon talking softly and playing a few games of cards until Stone felt himself tire again. The guys all said their good-nights, and to Stone's surprise, Preston kissed him gently on the lips.

"We'll be back tomorrow," Geoff said as he and Eli squeezed his hand before leaving the room.

"Do you have to go too?" Stone didn't want Preston to leave. He could hardly believe he was here, and quite frankly, he was afraid that if Preston left, he wouldn't come back. Not that he'd blame him after the way Stone had sent him away.

"I promised I'd be here and I will." Preston sat in the chair, and Stone closed his eyes, taking Preston's hand and allowing himself to sleep. He knew they had to talk and that he had a lot of explaining to do, but that could wait for now. Preston was here, and he'd take what he could get.

Stone woke a few times and always looked over toward the chair, seeing Preston's form curled up, asleep. He had to get him to stay. His heart didn't want him to leave, and this time he was going to follow it. Preston's head turned toward him, his eyes opening. "You should be asleep."

"I can't, Pres," he whispered very softly. The room and hallways were dim so everyone could sleep. "Are you gonna go back?" He swallowed, afraid of the answer.

"I talked to Robbie while you were asleep. He told me why you said I should take the job."

Stone suddenly felt cold. "He did?"

Preston moved the chair closer, his hand taking Stone's, his head resting against his arm. "Yeah. But I want to hear it from you."

"It's so hard. I was scared. You're a smart man, educated and brilliant. I'm just some hick from a pig farm. I was scared you'd get bored with me. And then I heard you taking to that farmer, working through all that financial mumbo-jumbo, and you sounded so excited. I couldn't ask you to stay and be a bank teller, not when you could be happy doing what you loved."

"So you pushed me away. Instead of asking me, you decided what I wanted." The heat in Preston's eyes scared Stone a little, and he tightened his grip on Preston's hand, hoping he wouldn't pull it away.

"I thought I had to let you go for your own good." Stone felt tears run down his cheek. "I know I was wrong, and I was miserable too, the entire time." Stone sniffed and wiped his eyes. "I thought it would get easier and that I would get over it, but I couldn't. Every night I'd think about you and wish you were with me." He heaved a breath between his tears. "I'm sorry I was so stupid." Stone buried his head in the pillow, unable to look Preston in the eyes anymore. He didn't want to see the anger and disappointment he felt sure were going to be there.

A hand smoothed through his hair, gently soothing away the fear. "We should have talked. I was miserable the entire time I was gone. Missing you and wondering why you sent me away." Stone turned back to look at him. "That last night…."

"I was making love to you because I thought it was the last time I'd get to, and I wanted you to know how I felt about you. That I loved you, even if I was too scared to say it." There, he'd finally told Preston how he felt. Now he looked deeply into his eyes, wondering if he'd be accepted or rejected.

"I should have told you I loved you too." Preston sighed just before kissing him again, this time harder and with all the feeling of newly declared love. "I should have demanded to know why you were sending me away. Instead, I was just shocked and hurt; I thought you didn't want me, like Kent." Preston rested his head right near his, leaning against the bed.

"I want you, Preston, arrogance and all." Stone petted the skin on Preston's arm.

"I promise to use it for good, Stable Boy." Preston winked at him, and Stone smiled. "My Stable Boy." The tone of his voice sent shivers through Stone, and he smiled as the one-time insult became an endearment. "You need to sleep."

"So do you." Stone didn't want to close his eyes; he was too happy and wanted to be awake to enjoy it. But his body had other ideas.

Stone woke and looked over at the chair, expecting to see Preston, but instead Eli was there, watching over him. "Where's Preston?" His stomach did a little flip. "He said he'd be here."

"He didn't leave, but I got the impression that there was something he needed to take care of. He'll be back." Food arrived, and Stone sat up and began to eat. "The doctor stopped by and said everything looks good, so you can go home this afternoon."

That was a relief. As he finished eating what he could of the bland food, Adelle walked into the room, carrying a bag. "How you feelin'?"

"They're trying to starve me with this stuff." He jabbed the spoon in some kind of cereal and it stayed there. "Who can eat this glop?"

She began to laugh. "Why do you think I brought you this?" Adelle placed the bag on the tray, and Stone tore into it, rewarded by the smell of homemade doughnuts. Digging into the bag, he started stuffing one into his mouth.

"Fank you," he mumbled around the mouthful of doughnut.

"You're welcome, Honey Child." She leaned closer, "But if you keep talkin' with your mouth full, I'll take them back with me."

Stone swallowed and did his best to look contrite. "Yes ma'am." The gleam in his eye gave him away.

"I understand that Preston's back." Adelle sat in one of the chairs, her back straight, coat draped over her lap.

Eli nodded before speaking. "He had to take care of something."

"Did he say what it was?" Stone asked, extremely curious, and that worried flutter in his stomach returned.

"No," Eli answered, "but he asked Joey to take him to his parents."

Love Means ... Freedom

CHAPTER 16

"DO YOU want me to go with you?" Joey asked as they pulled into Preston's parents' driveway.

"No." He looked at his friend and smiled. "Thank you, but this is something that I have to do on my own." He looked toward the front door as the car pulled to a stop. "It's time I finally did this for myself." Opening the door, Preston pulled out his walker and got to his feet, waving to Joey as the car pulled away before opening the front door and walking inside.

He found himself almost immediately engulfed in a hug from his mother. "Is he okay?" she whispered softly in his ear.

"He's going to be fine," he replied, grateful that he had her support, at least. "Is he home?"

She nodded, "Your father's in his office. He's been on the phone all day and getting grumpier by the minute. You know your being here isn't going to make him any happier," she warned. "You should have visited your friend and then gone back."

"I can't, and you know why. I love him, Mom, and that's not going to change." Preston made his way to a chair and sat, keeping the walker handy as he looked up at her, hoping, willing her to understand. He sure as hell knew that his father would never understand, but he figured she might.

"I know you do, and I just want you to be happy. That's the most important thing. But I worry. People will hurt you, maybe hate you for being... you know... gay. And no mother wants to see her child hurt."

"But you want me happy, right?" She nodded. "Stone makes me happy."

"But he sent you away," she protested.

"I know, Mom. He sent me away because he thought I'd be happier if I took the job." He reached for her hands. "Mom, he let me go because he didn't think he was good enough and that I'd be happier doing what I loved," he said earnestly, hoping she'd get the meaning.

Her mouth opened in surprise. "Are you saying he loved you enough to let you go for what he thought was your own good?" Preston nodded as she wiped her eye. "It must be wonderful to be loved that much." She looked longingly toward the office. "He used to love me like that." Before Preston could react to that glimpse into his parents' relationship, he was hugged within an inch of his life. "You deserve to be loved like that; we all do." He reached out to comfort her, and she stood back up and left the room, hurrying down the hall.

Listening to a door close, Preston got up and walked slowly toward his father's office, hearing him on the phone as he approached the door. His stomach tightened and his nerves went wild. This was something he knew he had to do. It was time. If he ever wanted to be free of him, he had to stand up to him. Without knocking, he turned the latch and pushed the door in, stepping into the room.

Preston's father was on the phone. "I'll call you back." They locked eyes as he hung up the phone. "What in hell are you doing here?" He stood up and glared at Preston.

His first instinct, after years of practice, was to step back, but he stopped himself. He could do this. "I came to visit a sick friend and to

Love Means ... freedom

talk to you." Preston used the walker to move forward, his steps becoming more confident as he got closer. "You've meddled in my life for the last time, Dad." He figured the best defense was a good offense. "I spent last night in the hospital with Stone, and we talked, for a long time. I know about your phone call to Stone, and I know how you feel about me. But I've decided that I'm going to live my life for me and not you."

"I'll cut you off." The old threat just didn't have the effect any more.

"I don't really care. I have friends and someone who loves me for me. I don't need you and I certainly don't need your job." Preston walked to the nearest chair and sat down, making himself comfortable, knowing that would frost his dad's butt. "By the way, since I'm a nice guy, I'll tell you that the head of finance in Kansas City is a complete idiot."

"Of course he's an idiot. I want you to take over for him!" Milford's eyes burned with fury and what Preston thought might be the beginnings of respect.

Preston smiled. "Not interested, Dad. I want to make it on my own." He softened his tone, "I don't want to be a success because you're my father. I want to be a success because you showed me I can do it on my own, just the way you did." Preston watched as his father plopped back in his chair.

"Is this really how you feel?" The expression was unreadable, but his voice held surprise rather than anger.

"Yes. I know I can do anything if I have Stone." His father's expression darkened visibly. "I know how you feel, Dad, but that's tough. I'm gay, I love Stone, and I'm going to be with him, if he'll have me. We've been through this before, and it's time you accept it." Preston stood up, using the walker to steady himself. Taking a few steps forward, he stood tall in front of his father's desk. "I will live my

169

life as I see fit. You can either be a part of it or not. That's up to you. But your interference will not be tolerated."

"You know I'm your trustee and that I can see to it that there's virtually nothing left of it."

"Well, Dad, I have four words for you: breach of fiduciary duty." Preston smiled. "I've already been in touch with a lawyer in town, and he's looking into how you've used that money." Preston stepped right up to the desk. "He's not pleased, and I'm sure he can get a judge to see that what you've been doing isn't according to the covenants of the trust." His father's eyebrows rose. "So you need to make it right and you need to turn it over to my lawyer, who'll act as trustee."

"You seem to have thought of everything," he said, clenching his teeth.

"Dad, you have a decision to make: you can either be a part of my life on my terms and accept me for who I am, or you can go to Hell!" Preston reached for the walker and, without another word, turned and began walking toward the door. He didn't turn around, and his father didn't say anything. "And by the way, the next time you call Stone, it had better be to tell him, 'Welcome to the family'." As he reached the door, he almost turned around, but he heard the phone ring. His father answered it, but there was definitely something different in his voice that Preston had never heard before.

Closing the door behind him, he felt light, free. His life was his own. Preston had no illusions that his father wouldn't still try to interfere, but the man had no power over him now, and it was time he lived his own life.

"Is it okay?" His mother met him in the hall.

"Everything's fine, Mom." He kissed her cheek. "Could you give me a ride back to the hospital?"

She nodded. "What are you going to do?"

Preston smiled, a big, bright smile. "I don't know, and it feels great. Best I've felt in a long time."

170

Love Means ... Freedom

"But you'll have nothing." She spoke softly with genuine concern.

"I won't have nothing, Mom. I'll have you and Stone and all the people at the farm. They accept me and care about me, even when I'm an arrogant ass." He could help smiling at his own use of Stone's words. "He loves me, Mom, and that means I'll have everything."

To his surprise, she hugged him, hard. "I'm proud of you." He rested his head on his mother's shoulder. "You probably think me an old fool, but I am so proud." She let him go. "You remind me so much of your father when we first met. He wanted to do it all on his own too." For a second, he thought he saw tears in his mother's eyes, but she turned away. "Get your coat and I'll take you to the hospital." She opened the closet door, getting her own, "Will you be back tonight?"

"I hope not, Mom." He smiled and got a wicked look from her in return. She walked out of the house and he followed her, moving slower, but under his own power. He got himself in the car, and she pulled out of the drive.

"What are you going to do about your stuff?"

Stone peered out the window, watching the white caps on the lake lifting the ice and letting it fall back again. "I'll fly back to Kansas City in a few days to get my things. I need to find a job and a place to live." He looked across the seat. "I'm not going to be staying at the house anymore. I need to be on my own." *God, that felt good to say.*

"I'm going to miss having you around." She sounded… lonely.

On impulse, he responded, "You could take riding lessons at the farm." He was being facetious, but saw her face brighten.

"Do you really think I could?"

"Of course. You can do anything you want," he responded, as she pulled the car into the hospital drive, stopping under the front portico. "I'll see you later, Mom." He leaned over the seat, kissing her on the cheek. "Thanks for everything. I'll let you know what's going on." He

171

unfolded the walker and got out of the car. "I love you, Mom." She smiled, a simple, happy smile that he hadn't seen in a while, and as he watched, she put the car in gear and drove away. Turning around, Preston walked into the hospital. A man greeted him and offered some help. "I'm okay." He smiled and made his way to the elevator and up to Stone's floor.

Stone was dressed and sitting on the edge of his bed. Geoff and Joey were there as well. "We were just waiting for you." Stone slipped off the bed, and an orderly appeared, helping him into a wheelchair.

"Would you like one as well, sir?"

Preston smiled. "No thanks. I've spent enough time in one of those to last a lifetime." He followed along behind the procession, making his way slowly back through the corridors and then down and out of the entryway. Geoff pulled his truck around, and Stone got in, with Preston sitting next to him, and Joey following in his own car. Pulling the door closed, Preston found himself leaning against Stone, his Stone. Extending an arm, he tugged him close, holding him the entire way back to the farm.

When they arrived, Preston got out and began walking toward the house, but Stone hurried toward the barn. "I'll be right in; I just have to check on Buster." Preston turned around and followed him. They both smiled when they reached the stall.

"If it's possible for a horse to look sorry...."

Preston had to agree. Buster seemed excited to see Stone, but tentative.

"You're a good boy." Stone rubbed his nose. "I know you didn't mean it."

"You should go inside. You just left the hospital and need to take it easy," Preston admonished lightly.

"Okay, Mom." Stone turned and smiled, making Preston's gut quiver with the heat, excitement, and love in that look. With a last pat, Stone said good-bye to Buster and put his arm around Preston's waist.

Love Means ... *Freedom*

Stone kept talking. "I'll help you, it's slippery." His hand around him felt so good, Preston couldn't help leaning into it. "I think we both need to get inside, preferably somewhere we can both rest."

Preston turned his head and found himself lip to lip with Stone.

"I missed you."

"I'm sorry you had to get hurt for me to see how much I love you."

"And I'm sorry I sent you away instead of just talking to you." Their lips met in a kiss that nearly buckled Preston's knees. "Let's get inside. Do you think you can make it up the stairs?"

"If you keep kissing like that, I'll sprout wings and fly up the stairs." Preston laughed and returned Stone's kiss before letting Stone guide him out of the barn and across the yard to the house. Adelle greeted them and insisted they eat something. Stone sat next to him, and they held hands through much of the meal, until Adelle shooed them out of the kitchen.

It took some doing, but Preston managed to get himself up the stairs and into Stone's bedroom. This time, there was no romantic disrobing and longing looks. Clothes were opened and dropped to the floor, with Stone slipping beneath the covers, and Preston following soon after. "You feel so good. I thought of this every night I was away." Preston brushed the hair out of Stone's eyes. "Thought about your eyes and your lips." He touched those lips with his thumb. "Remembered how you felt against me"—he let his eyes lower—"how you felt inside me."

"I thought about you too." Stone's hands slid along his chest, and Preston arched into the touch. He'd been longing for this for weeks, but he knew now was not the time.

"Should we be doing this? You just got out of the hospital?"

Stone leaned his head forward, capturing a nipple between his lips. "You're the best medicine I could have." Preston felt a hot tongue against his skin. "I love you."

Preston sat up and captured Stone's lips. "I love you too." He kept kissing. "I hate that we were apart, but it helped me realize just how much you mean to me." He released Stone's head and hugged him tight, pressing them together. Hell, he was trying to figure out how he could get even closer.

"I'm scared to close my eyes. I keep thinking you're a dream, and when I wake up, you'll be gone." Stone rested his head against Preston's shoulder, and he held him, sharing their warmth and just being close.

"I'm not a dream, and I'll be here, right here, when you wake up." Preston squeezed slightly, letting their heat mingle, his desire on simmer as he listened to Stone's breathing even out, and his lover slowly drifted off to sleep, with Preston not far behind.

He woke a few hours later to fading light outside the windows and a sleeping Stone still curled against him. Preston hated to move, but he had to. Moving slowly, he disentangled himself and made his way to the bathroom. Returning, he opened the door to find a very awake lover lying on his back, leaving no doubt about what he wanted. "Someone's awake."

Stone rolled over and patted the mattress, eyes heavy with desire. Preston rejoined him. Their lovemaking, fast and a little frenzied, was followed by slow, languid kisses that led to more kisses and still more lovemaking. Darkness outside the windows greeted the two lovers as they held each other, both spent and extremely happy. "Are you going back to Kansas City?"

"Just to get my things." Preston smiled as Stone's head found what was becoming a very familiar spot against his shoulder.

"What about your father?"

Love Means ... *Freedom*

"I told him what I was doing today." Preston ran his hands over Stone's hip as his big eyes shifted so they could see each other. "I don't really know what he thinks, but it doesn't matter. I'll get a job here, even if I have to work as a bank teller, and I'll find a place of my own to live."

"You could stay here." Stone curled closer, and he knew Stone was afraid again.

"Geoff and Eli don't need me living in their house with them, and I need my own place. Somewhere where we can be together"—he lowered his voice—"and get a little loud if we want to. I should be able to find someplace close. I'm not going to leave you, Stone."

Stone felt the tension lessen in his lover's body. "I was thinking," he offered as Preston's hand began tracing worried circles against his chest. "Maybe you could do for the other farmers what you did for that man before you left."

"What do you mean?" Preston was intrigued.

"Farming is a business, right?" There was a hint of excitement in Stone's voice.

"Yes. A specialized one, but a business nonetheless." Preston was curious what Stone was leading up to.

"A lot of farmers are people who've run things the way they have for years, and now they're having problems. So maybe you could work with them to help them be smarter about their money and how they run their businesses—sort of a financial planner for farmers." Preston didn't know what to say, except he wished he'd thought of it. "You could help them manage their money, help make sure they don't borrow too much, and maybe help them negotiate better rates with the banks… you know, stuff like that."

Preston was about to ask how Stone got so smart, but he knew. He grew up on a farm and knew the good and bad. "It could work. We can talk to Geoff about it later and see what he thinks."

"We?"

"Yeah. If I do this, I'll need to do it with you." The delight in Stone's eyes was matched only by the way he showed that delight. An hour later, Geoff's voice on the stairs calling them to dinner finally roused them from the bed.

The next morning, Stone was all smiles at breakfast, and Preston couldn't help returning his silly grin. "Now, you take it easy for a few days," Adelle warned lightly as she placed a huge plate in front of Stone. "I know you're hungry. Damn hospital food's bad enough to make anyone sick," she mumbled as she got more plates.

The phone rang once, and they continued eating. Stone shoveled it in like he hadn't eaten in a month, and Adelle looked on, grinning. The woman showed love with food and you reciprocated by eating.

"Stone, you have a call. Take it in the office if you'd like," Geoff said, as he took his place at the table next to Eli. Conversation circled about the day's chores and preparations for spring.

"If it ever shows up," Robbie grumbled.

"How could you possibly be cold?" Preston asked with a wicked smile. "You've got at least two shirts and a sweater on."

"I checked the Internet. It's seventy degrees in Mississippi," Robbie replied as Joey leaned close to Robbie's ear and said something, making Robbie blush. "Nah. I never would, you know that. But you gotta admit it's cold," Robbie added softly.

Preston turned away from the lovebirds and changed the subject. "I need to find a place to live and I was wondering if you know of anything. I want a place close by."

"I think there's a place for rent a ways up the road," Geoff replied between bites. "But you know you're welcome to stay here."

"Thanks." Preston was truly grateful. "But I don't think you need me in your house. Besides, after living with my folks, I think we need our own place."

"Our?" Geoff asked sheepishly. "I'll ask around."

Love Means ... Freedom

Preston looked around, wondering what was keeping Stone. His food was getting cold. Pushing his chair back, he grabbed his walker and followed a low voice into Geoff's office. Stepping into the room as Stone hung up, Preston saw he was visibly upset. "What is it?"

Stone looked lost. "It's my dad." He seemed dazed.

"What's he done? He's not trying to hurt you somehow, is he?" Preston could feel his temper rise.

Stone shook his head slowly. "Won't be doing anything again. He died."

CHAPTER 17

"YOU didn't have to do this." Stone looked out the window as the scenery passed in a blur.

"Yes, we did. You're family," Geoff replied from the driver's seat, as Stone felt Preston hug him closer. "We all know this is going to be hard for you, and we wanted to be there."

"But what about the farm?" Stone turned away from the window as Preston tugged him close, hugging tightly, protectively.

"The guys can handle things for a few days with Joey. Robbie canceled all the lessons and therapy sessions for the next few days, so just relax and don't worry about anything except getting through the meetings with the lawyer and the funeral." The truck bumped as Geoff flew over the roads.

"This isn't a race, Geoff," Eli said from the narrow back seat.

"Sorry." Geoff slowed down, but Stone paid no attention and let himself be comforted. Preston had been doing that every chance he got for the last few days, and Stone let him. He needed him, and he could hardly believe how Preston had been there for him.

Love Means ... Freedom

The miles of highway flew past, and before Stone wanted, they were pulling into the farm. Geoff turned off the engine, and they sat there breathing a collective sigh. "What first?"

"Mr. Halloran should be coming today to pick up the livestock." That had been the one thing Stone had been able to do besides arrange for the funeral. All the pigs had been sold, which was a huge relief. "I hate those fucking pigs," Stone mumbled as he opened the door. "I told him he had to load them." A truck and large trailer pulled up behind them. "Mr. Halloran, they're all yours."

The older man approached Stone and shook his hand. "I can't believe you're selling me the prize pigs."

"You'll take good care of them, and I hope you win as many ribbons with them as he did." Stone actually managed a smile.

"Let's get them loaded, boys," Halloran called, and the men backed the trailer to the hog barn and got to work.

"That's one thing down." Stone marched up to the front of the house, opening the door and going inside.

Looking around, not much had changed, except the house stank. "Jesus. It needs a good cleaning," Eli said behind him. "Let's get to it. I'll start in the kitchen. Is there anything you want?"

"No, when in doubt, pitch it. There isn't much I want, and I'll get that stuff loaded. The rest can either be sold or pitched. The lawyer said he'd sell anything that we left. If there's anything you want, take it." Stone kept his eyes from focusing on anything until he felt Preston's hand on his arm. "I never wanted you to see this place."

"Why? It's just a house."

"No, it's not. It's a hovel and it's terrible." Stone picked up a lamp and chucked it against the wall, glass shattering everywhere. "It's where he beat me and made me feel worthless." Stone turned around as Preston hugged him.

"You were never worthless." Preston lifted his chin. "To me you're everything." Stone felt warm and wanted as they stood there amid the remnants of a life he no longer wanted or had any use for. "Now let's get done so we can get the hell out of here."

"Yeah." Stone pulled away. "Can you throw away all the crap in here? I'm going to tear apart his bedroom."

"You got it." Preston grabbed a trash bag and began filling it as Stone walked down the hall to the last bedroom and pushed open the door. This room had been his mother's. His father had still used it, but it appeared to be the only room in the house that wasn't a shambles. Opening his box of trash bags, Stone opened the top dresser drawer and began emptying the contents.

Underwear, socks, and T-shirts all went into the trash. Slamming the drawer closed, Stone yanked open the next and began throwing old, tattered shirts one at a time, shaking each out before transferring it to the black trash bag. The final drawer was jammed with work pants. Knowing how lazy his dad could be about such things, he made sure to check the pockets before stuffing them in the bag as well.

At the back of the drawer, Stone found a wooden box. Gingerly lifting it out, he ran his hand over the smooth, polished wood. He knew what this was and tried keep himself from shaking with excitement.

"Stone, I've got the trash and junk out of the living room." He looked up at Preston leaning against the door frame for support.

"Where's your walker?" He leapt up and helped his lover to the bed.

"I didn't think I'd need it and I didn't." He seemed pleased. "Forgot about getting back, though."

Stone couldn't help smiling as he squeezed his lover, liking that he was nearby. "If I empty the closet, can you stuff the crap in garbage bags?"

"Sure, but shouldn't we donate this to someone?" Preston replied as Stone began slipping shirts off hangers.

Love Means ... Freedom

"God, no! Everything smells like pigs." Stone curled his nose, "Who'd want it?"

Preston sniffed. "Good point. Guess it proves you can get used to anything." Stone saw his lover wink at him before stuffing clothes into trash bags. Shirts, pants, shoes, old, forgotten, discarded things that Stone wouldn't touch with his bare hands, and a stash of half-empty liquor bottles went straight in the plastic bag.

"What's that box under the shelf?" Preston asked, pointing to the back corner.

Stone gingerly reached for it and pulled open the lid. "Jesus Christ!" He showed the contents to Preston. "There has to be thousands in here." Hundreds, fifties, and a few twenties filled the box.

"Put it aside for now."

"Should I give it to the lawyer?"

"Hell, no. Think of it as payment for years of free labor and abuse. Besides, it's yours anyway."

"I know, I just don't want…." He slipped the lid on the box and set it alongside the wooden box from the drawer.

"What's that?"

"It was my mom's." He ran a hand over the wood again and slowly lifted the lid. Looking inside, he gazed at a few pictures of himself as a baby and his mother standing next to a handsome man. He found some jewelry he remembered her wearing on top of a few letters. Lifting out the papers, he opened the envelopes and began to read. "These are from my father… my real father." He smiled and wiped away a tear. "They're love letters." Lifting out the last yellow paper, he opened the crinkled sheet. "Oh," he said as he handed it to Preston, his hands shaking.

"We regret to inform you of the death of Brandon Miller…" Preston read out loud. "It says he died saving the lives of others. He

181

was a hero, Stone." Preston refolded the paper. "We can look him up when we get back to the house."

Stone nodded and placed everything back in the box just as he found it. "Thank you."

"You're welcome, babe." They got back to work, digging through the room, getting it cleaned out. No other money or anything else of value surfaced, and Stone carried the bags out to the truck and threw them in the back, surprised at the number that were already in there.

Working for most of the afternoon, they cleaned out almost everything. The few things Stone wanted were packed up and loaded.

"What about the barn?" Geoff asked, standing by the recently emptied truck.

"There's some tack and things that someone might use. We could take it back and give it to any of Eli's students that could use it." Geoff patted Stone on the shoulder and ambled into the barn. Stone went back in the house to finish the last of it.

At the end of the day, the animals were gone, the house was emptied of the crap, and the rest would be sold along with the land and the house. The lawyer stopped by, and Stone signed the papers he needed to act as Stone's agent.

"Just the funeral tomorrow and it's over," Preston said as he held him.

"Yeah." Somehow he knew it wouldn't be that easy.

Stone walked into the small church up the road from the farm. He didn't look at the urn or the few flowers. Taking Preston's hand, he slipped into a pew and waited for the service to begin.

People dribbled in the doors, a few offering their condolences, but most just taking a seat. This was a small community, and his father talked, so he figured everyone knew what had happened, or at least his old man's side of it. Not that he cared anyway. After today, he wasn't coming back.

Love Means ... *freedom*

The minister began the service, and Stone listened absently, doing his perfunctory duty and no more. There were no tears and just a few coughs as the service wound to its conclusion. Stone was eternally grateful to be surrounded by friends, and friends who treated him more like family than his own had ever done.

A final prayer was offered by the minister, followed by an "Amen," and Stone slowly released the breath he felt like he'd been holding since he'd gotten the phone call a few days earlier.

The minister greeted everyone solemnly at the door. "I'm sorry for your loss," he said, and Stone nodded mutely, not knowing what else to do or say. It was over.

"Are you ready to go home?" Geoff asked, and Stone found himself smiling for the first time in days.

"Almost. There's just one last thing I have to do." Stone walked down the steps and waited. He'd heard the voice he was listening for behind him. Looking toward the door, he saw Uncle Pete shake hands with the minister before descending the stairs.

"You hurt me, you bastard!" Stone gritted out between clenched teeth. "I came to you for help and you hurt me!" Pete opened his mouth, and Stone balled his fist, drew his arm back, and punched the man in the jaw with everything he had. "Stay away from me, or so help me, I'll cut your balls off," Stone growled as Pete collapsed like a rag doll into the snow, the minister looking in open-mouthed shock.

"Now I'm ready to go home."

CHAPTER 18

PRESTON watched the lights flash by the windows. Eli snuffled from the back seat, having fallen asleep a while ago, and Stone leaned against his lover, the adrenaline from his pugilistic encounter long worn off. His eyes were closed, lips slightly parted, expression relaxed and Preston suppressed the urge to kiss him, content to hold him. Preston swore that Stone hadn't slept more than a few hours since they left for Petoskey days earlier.

"They're both out," Geoff half whispered from the driver's seat.

"Have been for a while." Preston felt Stone burrow closer and settle again. "They both worked hard."

Geoff nodded slowly. "They always do." The truck switched lanes and passed a slower car. "Have you given any more thought to finding a place to live?"

"You're leaving?" Stone shifted in his arms, suddenly looking up at him.

"I have to get my things from Kansas City, but I'd asked about finding a place nearby," he said lightly, and felt Stone relax against him again. "I was hoping I could find a place that we could share." Stone turned again, this time his eyes shining with almost happy disbelief.

"Right now, there isn't much, but things usually open up in the spring." Geoff reached over to Stone and squeezed his shoulder. "Stay at the house until you find a place." Geoff smiled and returned to his driving. "You're both family." Preston felt himself smile and relaxed against the seat. He'd found a place where he was accepted; they both had.

They rode quietly until the truck pulled into the farmyard. The roughening of the ride roused both Eli and Stone, both of them stretching as the truck came to a stop. Getting out, Preston made his way into the house using the walker while the others unloaded the truck.

Adelle fussed over all of them as they entered. "Sit down, I'll have some dinner ready shortly." Preston didn't argue, and she brought him a mug of hot cocoa, with the others entering a few minutes later. More mugs seemed to materialize on their own as the others sat down quickly, followed by heaping plates of Adelle's famously wonderful fried chicken. Conversation was minimal, with Geoff insisting that Adelle join them. It was something she rarely seemed to do, but Geoff had been working to convince her that she was a member of their little family just like everyone else.

After dinner, Adelle cleaned up her kitchen, and Preston followed Stone up to bed, navigating the stairs on his own. Preston went right to the bathroom, cleaning up before heading back to the bedroom, where he expected to find Stone already asleep. Instead, he found his lover wide-awake and naked, lying on top of the covers.

"Get in, you'll be cold." Stone slid under the blankets, and Preston joined him, with Stone pulling them together. "I appreciate everything you've done."

"I didn't do much."

"You were there; that was more than enough." Stone kissed him, rolling him onto his back and pinning him to the mattress. "I love you."

Preston would have responded, but Stone kissed him hard enough to suck the words from his mind.

"I thought you were tired." Not that he was complaining.

"Slept in the car." Stone pulled on his bottom lip.

"I see." Preston tugged Stone closer, intensifying the kiss as he sucked on Stone's tongue.

"I want you."

"You have me."

Stone pulled back, locking his gaze onto Preston's. "No, I want you. Want you to love me."

Preston stilled. "Are you sure?" Stone nodded, and Preston stroked a lightly stubbled cheek. "I don't want to hurt you."

"You'd never hurt me, that I know."

Preston wasn't sure and nearly demurred, but the love in Stone's eyes drove away his fears. Rolling them on the bed, Preston stroked Stone's skin lightly. "You don't have to do this. You have nothing to prove to me. Nothing at all."

"I'm not proving anything to anyone, except that I love you."

"Roll over," he whispered into Stone's ear as he reached to the nightstand. After grabbing the supplies, he turned back to Stone and gasped slightly at what seemed to him to be acres of pale, smooth, perfect skin. "I missed you." Preston leaned forward, kissing a trail along Stone's shoulder and down his back. "You taste so good." He let his hand slide over the curve of Stone's butt and felt him shiver slightly. "Does that feel good?"

"Uh-huh." Stone thrust his butt up, and Preston slid his fingers along his cleft, lightly skimming over the skin. Slicking a finger, he lightly touched his lover's entrance, watching for any sign of discomfort or anxiety, and instead he got a deep, low sigh. That sound sent a zing down his spine that settled in his groin, making him throb against the sheets. Preston had to keep telling himself to go slowly.

Love Means ... Freedom

As slowly as his clouded mind would allow, Preston slid a single finger into his lover, curling it slightly. "Preston!" He smiled at Stone's ragged cry, and did it again. "What are you doing to me?" He stopped, afraid he was hurting him. "Please don't stop, don't ever stop."

Smiling to himself, he added a second finger, his dick throbbing with every sound Stone made. Those sounds went right to the heart of his desire. He loved this man with everything he had, and he wanted to show him just how big that love was.

"Please, Preston."

"Shh. Don't wanna hurt you." He was trying to be as careful as he could.

Propping himself up on his hands, Stone arched his back and angled for a kiss. Their lips met, and Preston rubbed the special spot again. Stone cried out into the kiss. Positioning himself as best he could, Preston rolled on a condom. The heat of his lover's body threatened to burn his as he breached the outer muscle. "Stone." The smooth heat threatened to fry his brain. This was Stone, the man he loved.

Sinking deeper, he heard Stone cry out and thrust against him, stealing his breath in a flash of tight heat. Sinking deep, he stopped and waited. "Preston, please...." Taking the plea as permission, he began to move slightly.

"Love you, Stone." He thought his head was going to explode. Thoughts of what this meant flooded through Preston. The level of trust and love it took for Stone to give himself like this reached deep into Preston's heart. Moving carefully, he concentrated on Stone's pleasure, listening to the small noises and cries. Stone's last experience had been traumatic, and it warmed Preston's heart every time Stone moaned softly and pushed against him. He could feel small ripples running through the younger man with each movement they made. Leaning forward, he nuzzled Stone's neck, thrusting deep and stilling. "You, Stone Hillyard, are the sexiest man I've ever met."

187

Preston could hear Stone's deep breathing as he began thrusting deeper. Stone's groans continued and built, unintelligible cries of encouragement and passion that communicated all Preston needed to know. "Preston, love you!!!!" Stone cried out as his body gripped Preston like a vice. He knew Stone was coming, and the image was enough to send him over the edge as well.

"Stone." Preston opened his eyes again, realizing he was splayed on top of his lover. "Am I hurting you?" He didn't want to move. Their bodies were still joined, and he wanted to stay that way as long as he could.

Stone wriggled against him. "No. You feel good." Preston began nibbling on Stone's ear, and he began to giggle a little. "You're tickling." Preston felt their bodies separate with a small mutual moan. "It's so good to hear you laugh." Preston rolled gently onto the bed. "I like the sound of your laugh."

"I have lots to be happy about: you, a new family, a home, and I feel free. Free of a bastard father and free of the…." Stone's voice fell away, but Preston knew exactly what he meant and how he felt.

Preston put his arms around Stone's chest, hugging Stone's back to his chest. "It's wonderful, isn't it? Being free." They could both live their lives and build one together.

"Free to love." Stone rolled over in Preston's embrace. "Free to love you forever."

Love Means ... *Freedom*

EPILOGUE

"STONE." He heard Preston's excited voice from inside Geoff's office. "I found something." He walked inside and saw Preston sitting in Geoff's chair, with Geoff peering over his shoulder.

"Are you two still at it? I thought we'd given up on that already." Preston looked down his nose at him, and Stone chuckled softly. He should have known that he wasn't about to give up. Walking into the room, he stood in front of the desk. "Did you find something?"

"Better." Preston looked up, a grin on his face. "I sent an e-mail to the Marines. It seems they've been looking for you." Preston turned the monitor around.

"They want me to contact them." He looked up, confused, which only increased when he saw the goofy smiles on their faces. "I take it you have an idea why."

"On a hunch based upon the letter in the box from your mother, I looked further. It seems your father died under fire, saving the lives of seven other men. So I contacted the Marine Corps and told them about you and that you were his son and so on. I sent them copies of the letters and the letter telling your mother about his death." Preston looked up from the screen. "It seems that your father was posthumously

189

awarded the Silver Star, and the Marine Corps has been looking for a relative to present it to all these years."

"You mean me?" Stone could hardly believe it.

"Yes. They need proof, and we'll find it." Preston got up and walked around the desk, still a little unsteady, but definitely walking on his own. "You don't have anything of your father, but you will. Look...."

"Is that him?" Stone found himself staring at the picture on the computer screen. He recognized the eyes and chin.

"Yes. You look like him." Preston and Geoff both grinned like idiots.

"Wow," Stone mumbled as he committed the picture to memory.

"I hate to break this up, but Jasper will be here soon, and you"— he looked at Preston—"have a riding session scheduled."

"Do you need the walker?" Stone asked. Preston had been using it less and less, mainly for longer distances.

"No. Jasper says I've used it long enough and it's time I stand on my own two feet, so to speak." Preston grinned, his eyes twinkling. "I've been waiting for that pronouncement ever since the accident."

"We should celebrate." Stone leered slightly at his lover.

"Celebrate later, you two," Geoff admonished with a smile, "or you won't have time for riding." Geoff left the office.

Stepping carefully, Stone watched as Preston walked slowly through the house. "You have a great butt, you know that."

"You said that last night too," Preston quipped as he slipped on a heavy jacket. Stone steadied Preston as they walked across the farmyard. He could feel Preston's legs wobble a little as they walked, but he knew how much this meant to his lover.

"The trees look ready to pop open." Stone pointed to the large oak in the back yard. "Oh, look, the tulips have opened. I always love spring." Stone took a deep breath. "And not a hint of pig."

"Me, too, but you have to admit, it was a pretty amazing winter." Preston stopped walking and turned to him, kissing him softly. "Best winter I can remember."

A car pulled to a stop in the yard. "Break it up, lovebirds." Car doors thunked closed.

"Sadist," Preston teased as Jasper and Derrick walked toward them.

"No more walker?" Derrick asked with a huge smile.

"Nope. I've been given permission to dump it, except for going up and down stairs." Preston had already donated his wheelchair to a local nursing home.

"We just need to strengthen your legs a little more," Jasper explained as they all walked toward the barn.

Belle's head bobbed with excitement as Preston made his way to her stall. He'd graduated to a more challenging ride a few weeks earlier, but he never forgot to bring her a treat, and she knew it. "How's my girl?" Preston cooed, and the others rolled their eyes.

"I never thought I'd see the day when Preston Harding would kiss a horse," Jasper teased.

"I didn't kiss...." Preston coughed and sputtered as Belle stuck out her tongue, looking for another treat, and slobbered all over Preston's face. "Belle..." Preston whined as he wiped his face, sputtering and coughing, trying to remove the horse spit from his mouth. "Gross."

Stone doubled over, holding his sides. "I swear, I've heard of a horse laugh, but I never *saw* one laugh before." Stone almost fell on the floor he was laughing so hard.

"It wasn't that funny." Preston tried to keep a straight face, but couldn't hold it more than two seconds. "Okay, maybe it was." The laughter died down, and Stone saddled his horse, leading him toward the ring. Preston mounted from the raised platform, surprised to see both Jasper and Derrick mounted and ready, joining Joey and Robbie as they rode double, with Robbie laughing as he hung onto Joey.

"Geoff, are you and Eli joining us?" Stone called as he led Buster into the ring.

"We'll be ready in a few minutes," Geoff replied as he walked around the edge of the ring.

"What's going on? I thought this was a therapy session." Preston began looking around, wondering if he'd missed something.

"We're all going for a ride," Geoff explained as he pulled the large doors open. "Just give us a minute and we'll join you."

Stone trotted up next to Preston and smiled over at him. "Your first trail ride."

"Where are we going?"

"Don't know. Geoff thought it would be good to get outdoors." Stone looked over at his lover sitting tall in the saddle, legs curled around the chestnut gelding, remembering having those legs curled around him the night before. "Shit," he murmured to himself. His errant body had sprung to life, and he needed to cool off; riding with a hard-on could be painful. Geoff and Eli joined the group, and they moved out, leaving the enclosed ring and moving into the spring sunshine.

Stone followed behind Preston, paying as much attention to his lover's bobbing backside as he did to his horse. Derrick trotted up and fell in near both of them. "So when are you moving into your own place?"

"Next week." Stone grinned widely. They'd bought a small home that had once been a one-room schoolhouse. It even had a small tower with a bell. "I'm so excited." They'd pooled their money, including the cash Stone had found when cleaning out the house, to buy the house together.

"I'll bet you are." Derrick smiled.

"It's even got a small room Preston can use as an office." Preston had begun offering his financial planning expertise to the local farmers, and word had spread. "He has two appointments this afternoon." There were times he thought he was going to burst with pride.

"I've heard he's getting clients from around the county."

"The college contacted him to see if he'd be interested in teaching some classes."

"Sounds like things are working out."

"They are, for the most part." Preston's mother was great and called regularly, but his father barely spoke to him. And the one time he and Stone had met, he'd ignored Stone completely, which only made Preston angry. But Stone could care less. He had everything he could want: a home, someone who loved him, and an adopted, extended family. He smiled to himself. *Hell, he even had someone to mother him.*

Preston slowed his horse, allowing Stone to catch up. "You look about ready to burst." Preston's own eyes shone with delight.

"So do you." They'd talked about little but plans for their new house for the last month.

"I'm just excited about our place."

"I know, a home of our very own." Stone motioned for Preston to stop, and he did the same. Leaning over, he captured his lover's lips.

"Have you given any thought to what we talked about yesterday?" Stone nodded and chewed on his bottom lip. "You don't have to, but I know you'll do well."

"Do you really think I'm cut out for college?"

Preston slipped a hand into Stone's. "You're cut out to do whatever you want. You could start with a few classes in the fall." Stone wasn't sure what to say. "I know you're nervous about it." Preston smiled. "I'll tell you a secret—I was scared to death as a freshman."

"You? Mr. Arrogant?" Stone teased, knowing Preston's arrogance had been nothing more than a cover for his fears.

"Yes, me." Preston chuckled.

"Okay."

The group turned back toward the barn, racing across the field. Stone and Preston held hands as their horses lazily walked them home. "You'll do it?"

"Yeah." The last of his fears fell away. Together, they could do anything. Preston let go of his hand. "Go on, I know you want to. I'll be in shortly." Stone smiled and spurred Buster on, letting him run, the two of them flying across the field together. Buster needed to feel free too.

ANDREW GREY grew up in western Michigan with a father who loved to tell stories and a mother who loved to read them. Since then he has lived throughout the country and traveled throughout the world. He has a master's degree from the University of Wisconsin-Milwaukee and works in information systems for a large corporation. Andrew's hobbies include collecting antiques, gardening, and leaving his dirty dishes anywhere but in the sink (particularly when writing). He considers himself blessed with an accepting family, fantastic friends, and the world's most supportive and loving partner. Andrew currently lives in beautiful historic Carlisle, Pennsylvania.

Visit Andrew's web site at http://www.andrewgreybooks.com and blog at http://andrewgreybooks.livejournal.com/. You can e-mail him at andrewgrey @comcast.net.

Love Means… by ANDREW GREY

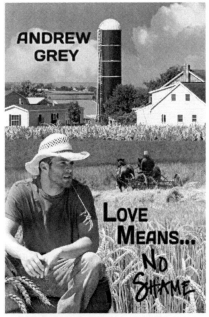

http://www.dreamspinnerpress.com

Contemporary Romance by ANDREW GREY

Contemporary Fantasy by ANDREW GREY

Lightning Source UK Ltd.
Milton Keynes UK
UKOW041812110712

195831UK00011B/141/P